Coffee Maidz

New Beginnings

Zoanna Valund

Bayview Publishing Qld

This book is dedicated to all the hard working baristas and cafe owners on the Gold Coast, Australia. The coffee, atmoshere and stories help inspire me to write this book. It may not reflect every cafe or the personalities of those who work there but Im sure some will recognise the circumstances and the hopes of all small busness's

Contents

CHAPTER 1

---◆◇◆---

SUMMERTON

T he streets are almost empty as Katie rode her old push bike through the quiet suburban street of the small town of Summerton. After the mills closed, the town became abandoned, until some Hi-tech Corporation whizz kids moved to town. Other businesses had sprung up and the small town was fast becoming gentrified. The added prosperity had helped the locals and Katie had found work as a Barista in a local café.

Katie, in her mid-20's with slight build but nice figure which she kept through riding and the occasional swim in the nearby ocean. Her friend and fellow barista, Alice often told her she could do with a makeover as there was an underlying Latin beauty that she needed to bring out. But that was not in Katies thoughts at all. She wanted out and an education but her financial situation precluded that.

Despite that she had a hidden beauty that customers had noticed. Her ample bust, flowing fair hair and long legs often turned heads when she swam at the nearby beach and made her tip tray better than average at her second job in a sleazy pole dancing club downtown.

Katie had always been shy, never had a real boyfriend or relationship but deep down she yearned for a true relationship and happiness. She had once planned to go to law school but she had neither the grades nor the money. She left school early to help support her parents whose health had deteriorated. She accepted that her life involved working in a job making coffee daily. This was not what she had planned for her future but dropping out of school to help her folks seemed like the only choice.

Upon their passing, she inherited substantial medical debts and little else, aside from the deteriorated family residence located in the less affluent area of town. She was stuck with little education, and the need to earn what she could with what she knew best, coffee, this seemed her only choice and the only thing she felt confident about.

From an early age she had travelled with her father and mother who were coffee and tea buyers. She knew her beans and how to make a good cup of coffee. She cycled down the quiet streets in the early morning sunlight, observing the changes that had taken place in her town.

Summerton was an old Mill town full of empty buildings and factories which had long since moved overseas. Taking their workers with them. Tax and incentives from other countries made it imperative for Companies to move their mills to survive. Summerton was known for its fabrics, carpets, and other products, along with its coastal location, which attracts tourists.

The coastal location included a port, heavily used until the factory closed and the branch line shut down. After that the town fell into disarray until the hi-tech industries saw the advantages and began to revive the town and its abandoned buildings. Downtown Somerton improved after renovations and the port expanded.

Corruption

During the town's regeneration, the mayor and his siblings acquired properties for financial gain. John Grumbleton, a relative of the mayor, will oversee the diner's renovation to meet changing customer preferences. The building also came with an adjoining bakery that had been dormant for years.

Several historical homes close to the city centre have been bought and renovated by corporate executives. The old mill's administrative building is now a renovated office. This attracted people such as lawyers' doctors and dentists into the town.

The town's peripheral areas, which had long remained undeveloped, were transformed into residential estates to accommodate incoming workers. This attracted other groups to support the growing town. Multiple companies regarded the railhead and access to the main highway as advantageous for their operations. And so, the town had grown.

Cycling through the refurbished downtown area Katie waved to a friendly delivery man and regular at the café as she passed the refurbished buildings and up market stores that had sprung up. The town had gone from abandoned to prosperous in the last 5 years. Katie grew up in the town and knew it well. Distracted by a car horn she waved back to her friend and fellow barista Alice as she motored past in her old car.

Alice had moved to Somerton after a divorce in another state and had settled into the lifestyle in the new age, Somerton. At Grumbles Café (as it was known by the locals). Katie felt fortunate to have Alice beside her. Alice was a very experienced barista and meticulous in her understanding of the coffee that she made and taught. Katie did tricks and saw Alice as a kind of mother figure even though she was a bit rough around the edges.

Katie found their relationship the only worthwhile thing she had and Alice inspired her in all aspects of coffee. This was to be an utterly new age for Grumbles Cafe. Even though John Grumbleton had extraordinarily little to do with its running of it, as Alice was the real driver behind the changes that had made the cafe popular and the place to be for the best coffee in town. Alice, Katie, and the two servers frequently worked part-time at various large events hosted by entrepreneurs due to their reputation for quality coffee and service.

CHAPTER 2

GRUMBLES CAFÉ

Peddling down the side road she sees Alice pulling into the dead-end lane that ran behind the small group of shops and The Coffee Stopz Café known to most as Grumbles. The old diner looked like a dump due to minimal exterior maintenance. It was a different matter inside where Alice and Jeremy (a server) had transformed it from a greasy diner to a hip café. Alice had stolen the furniture from the abandoned buildings and together with Jeremy's talent for decoration and a local graffiti artist the interior was bright and entertaining. The booths and a long counter were replaced by café tables and even a couple of sidewalk tables.

The old Coffee machines were useless but Alice kept them going and did all the repairs herself. Grumbleton seldom paid for anything and spent the occasional time he was at the café fiddling around in the storeroom. Jeremy, a baker by trade and his partner wanted to open the old bakery and knock down the adjoining wall to make the place a true bakery. Grumbleton refused to allow this let alone put up any money.

The penny-pinching owner, John Grumbleton, had strange habits and a poor attitude toward his staff. He refused to spend any money on the place, and it showed. The café was poorly managed because the owner lacked expertise. It was the coffee skills of Alice and Katie and the personalities of the servers that brought the customers to this bohemian café down a side street behind the main buildings.

Grumbleton is in his late 50's, overweight and balding. Everyone saw him as a dirty old man that used threats to control and manipulate his staff. He was obsessed with stock control which he used to give the impression that he was a part of the place, but everyone knew who really ran the show. known for the best coffee in town it attracted young professionals to the place. Her fellow Barista Alice, a mid-40's divorcee, was a good friend and good barista as well. They worked well together and enjoyed upsetting old Grumbles.

Katie pulled into the dead-end lane as Alice was getting stuff out of her car. As usual the back alley was the best place to park. Katie chained her bike, took the bag from the basket, and walked to Alice, who was rummaging in her old, un-likely-to-be-stolen car.

"Morning Katie" said Alice in her usual upbeat way as she locked her car and they walked around the corner to the side entrance they find Grumbles emptying the waste bins from behind the counter.

"Good morning, Alice, Katie, I want to see you both before you start" said Grumbles with a tone of authority in his voice. Katie looking bemused at Alice wondered what his problem was this time, and it was most unusual to see him in the place before opening.

."What for, were not late "says Alice looking quizzical.

The prompt reply made Katie step back as Grumbles got into Alices face who didn't move an inch.

"You're not late sweetheart. But you know how he works. You've both had warnings before and I want to know what is happening to my special cookies, have you been handing out my special cookies again? I came in early to check the bins and by my tally we are at least one box down and the bins are full of them.

Alice gets right up to him and says. "They're in the bin because nobody eats the horrible things so we have to throw them out."

Grumbles backs away talking as he leaves the café.

"Okay I don't accept that excuse and I will be watching you both and those servers so you know my rule of one cookie per cup of premium blend Coffee."

"Fine" says Alice, "we will make sure we follow your rules and keep throwing away your profits if that's what you want."

Waving his finger at them as he exits the side door with Katie holding it open, Grumbles has a parting shot. "It's not good enough. I will review the CCTV footage and make sure you're not giving it out with regular cups. These things cost money you know."

Katie's eyebrows raised goes to close the door but Grumbles holds it open and moves closer to her in an intimidating fashion. "As for you missy if it happens again, I will be taking it out of your pay or in some other way" he says leering at her.

Katie, feeling threatened and assaulted by Grumbles closeness and bad breath, let us go of the door and pushes past him.

Alice moves in quickly. "That's enough of that" she says pushing the door shut on Grumbles, we'll look after your awful cookies.

Having had his moment of pleasure for the day, he reinforces the dominance he leaves walking through the door. "You'd just better do that." He says walking off down the street to his car. With his clipboard and packet of special biscuits.

Alice turns to Katie who is a little shaken, You Okay kiddo she says putting her arm around her as Jeremy and his partner come in.

"What's happened" says Jeremy. "We just past Grumbles walking down the street muttering to himself."

"Nothing to worry about" says Alice. "The bastard was just doing his usual intimidation routine about those stupid biscuits his auntie makes and then he upset Katie as he was leaving."

"Biscuits, and cookies again" says Jeremy, "what's his obsession with those horrible things."

"You know what he is like just pile the uneaten ones up and put them on his desk in the storeroom at the end of the day and Katie and I will put a tally of the "special coffees" we make to go with them." Says Alice

The morning setup goes smoothly without Grumbles constant interference. Alice is busy operating the tired old coffee machine for the first brew of the day as she sets up cups and checks the order tabs. Looks like it's going to be busy today, Katie is setting up the other old machine and cleaning down the counter.

"I think so", says Katie, "Here come the regulars" noting the first customers heading toward the counter they had a regular list of what individuals preferred along with a photo and names as well as the personal coffee mugs they had sold and engraved with their names that sat behind the counter.

Katie enjoyed working with Alice and found her forthright and outspoken ways entertaining. They were a highly efficient team with Jeremy catering for the sit-down customers it ran like clockwork. Customers appreciated being addressed by name and having their coffee prepared promptly, allowing them to cross the street and enter the rear entrances of the buildings where they were employed. It was also a great break spot as they could sneak out the back and across the street to the café.

Alice was certainly a character. She was buxom and attractive in a sexy kind of way. She had a teenage daughter from a failed marriage to a lawyer who she met in school and married young. Giving up her chance of an education to support him through law school and raising their daughter he left her for a younger woman. This left Alice with few choices of a career so she fell back on what she knew, making coffee.

Katie found Alice to be street smart but quite articulate having read quite extensively. Surviving in the city is where her career as a barista was formed and she worked in some of the best restaurants and coffee houses. She once explained that the alimony helped but they rarely saw her former husband after the breakup. This left her damaged emotionally and she found she could use sex to get what she wanted and often did with no remorse. She appreciated the company of men and understood social interactions well.

Katie found her motherly and was always trying to guide her, but this sometimes-annoyed Katie and caused friction between the two. John Grumbleton knew that his team ran the cafe and were the reason for the current success of the place and was loath to push his luck and have them walk out but as with most cowardly bullies he liked to stand over them.

Katie looked up from her machine noting that Jeremy and his partner Nigel were much more than servers. Their friendly service style, remembering the names of the regulars and their favourite brew as well as asking about life in general made the place what it was. They both loved Alice and Katie and the whole team was a town favourite with the customers who enjoyed their banter and back chat of Grumbelton. Jeremy was gay of course and very much in love with his partner Nigel. They both hoped to open the old bakery next door but Grumbles who owned both was having none of it despite continuous pleas by both men.

"Special Cookies for the desk Ogre "says Nigel. "Only one bite taken so perhaps Grumbles could finish this plate off." Emptying the plate into zip bag with the receipt for the 2 special coffees she plonks them on the back counter.

"I should ram the things down his nasty old throat "says Alice smiling demurely making a rude gesture,

"no one likes the horrible things except him. That is why I give them away to the homeless guy down the back alley? He is the only one apart from the cats that eat the things and I'm not sure he eats them or sleeps on them."

Katie smiles, "Okay but how do you hide the numbers."

"Easy" says Alice He get me to do the orders of the bloody things. I changed the order and put the stock away so he thinks he has 5 packs when in fact he has 6. The other pack goes to the homeless guy with some other leftovers. The packaging is great for preserving stuff so the homeless guys use it for their food and stuff."

Overhearing the bit about sleeping on them, Jeremy returning with empty cups pauses. "No chance of that sweetie. They're too hard to use as a mattress and too unpleasant to eat so maybe he uses them for bathroom stuff." He makes a sweeping motion past his behind.

"Actually" says Alice "he uses them for fuel in his little burner stove."

The giggling begins and becomes infectious causing customers to look. One of the regulars asks, "what's the joke guys?"

Alice still giggling tells him about the cookie thing and the customer laughs with them. "By the way, does anybody eat those things? I've never tasted anything as bad and thank God you've got those shortbread things to go with them on the same order." He says.

"Anyway, where's old Grumbles today?" the customer asks.

"I think he said he was getting his car serviced" says Katie.

Alice, in a muffled voice next to Katies ear. "He needs fucking servicing, might improve his demeanor, pity his poor wife."

Sometime later after the early rush is over there is a knock on the rear door. Alice opens the door to Brad the coffee services delivery guy. He is a 40 something rugged looking guy in company uniform with a pleasant attitude and personality. "I hope you remembered my order of premium blend and the free Cookie bonus that comes with that," says Alice smiling.

Brad opens a box to show her the special cookies. Smiling and winking as he opens the box. "I certainly did. Here's Mr. Grumbleton, boxes of Cookies, shall I put it all in the storeroom ladies" he says smiling broadly as he wheels the supplies into the storeroom.

Alice nods casually. "Just the usual brew Brad, how's your day so far."

Looking up from putting the supplies on the storeroom shelf he smiles

"All the better for seeing you two lovely ladies." Grumbles return through the side door and overhears the last part of the conversation.

"Don't forget to pay, this is not a charity shop," says Grumbles passing the counter.

Brad hands over five dollars and makes a face whilst he talks under his breath to Katie. "Could have fooled me, looks like a charity shop," smiling at Katie. Who flashes a shy smile back at Brad as Alice gets his coffee ready.

"It's about time you tried something else Brad. Let me make you my Colombian Latte" says Alice.

Grumbles yelling from the back room.

"You'll have to drink that in the staff room; there's a good fellow."

Brad, speaking quietly to Katie. "Ah yes, the staff room, that greasy little table and chairs spot at the back of the storeroom where the cockroaches have their dances."

Grumbles looking around the corner of the storeroom with an abusive look on his face.

"You got a problem with that!"

Brad smiling nicely, "no, why, do you think I'll upset the cockroach's morning meeting?"

Grumbles frowning. "What are you lot smirking about? Get back to work."

Jeremy returning to the counter with an order raises his voice as he approaches so Grumbles can hear. I wonder if Grumbles knows his flies are open. There is the sound of someone falling over and things falling and cursing swearing. The collective group all giggle and Brad retreats to his van with his Coffee. The Ladies fuss with the coffee machine while Jeremy waves special Cookies under his nose in a disdainful manner as he departs to clean a table.

Still fumbling with his flies, Grumbles heads toward the back door. Announcing he will be out for a few hours so they'll have to hold the fort whilst he is gone. Alice is quick off the mark to reply. "Okay boss, enjoy your massage! Have a happy ending," flashes a naughty smile at Grumbles as he leaves. Grumbles muttering as he leaves, bloody women to himself knowing he must put up with their jibes as they are the core of his pathetic business.

The morning rush over and cups cleaned ready for the lunchtime surge, Katie is busy grinding beans and cleaning down the old machines whilst Alice checks the till and counter. Holding up a brochure she has kept under the counter, Alice turns to Katie.

"Hey Katie, about this Baristas competition I mentioned are you in or not?" Katie, still busy with the machines replies, not likely at this stage Alice, funds are tight, it's in another state and old Grumbles isn't likely to give us both time off together.

Alice moves closer, her hands on her hips. "Defeat begins when you doubt yourself." Leave Grumbles to me. If you are concerned about the money, I have saved enough from my alimony for our travel expenses and accommodation. All you need to do is say yes. Smiling like a Cheshire cat and up close to Katie's face she repeats the question. "The answer is yes, ok, yes right!" Katie smiled and tried not to laugh at Alice's gestures and cross-eyed look. "Okay, okay, you win but I don't expect we will do any good."

Alice stands back with a hand on her forehead. "There you go again. You're so negative, no wonder you haven't hooked a man yet." Katie looking hurt responds quickly. "Now that hurts Alice. I suppose I should be more like you, is that what you're saying? I should sleep with every man I meet; smoke dope shows off my assets like your fake breasts. Wasn't it you who wanted us to go to work across town in that topless coffee shop that closed last year because it was in front of a knocking shop? What about that young guy you were dating? He looked more like your son."

Alice feigning hurt, turns away, smiling to herself secretly. Katie, that hurts. I thought we were friends. I never knew you felt that way." Katie realizes she was a bit brash. "I'm sorry Alice. I didn't mean it; I'm a bit down today and Grumbles didn't help my mood."

Alice puts an arm around Katie. "It's okay kiddo, I'm kidding, I know things have been tough for you too and working in this dump doesn't help. I'm sure you will get back to school one day and meet a nice young fella and have kids and all the other stuff. My life is not a model to be proud of and your right, I do sleep around a bit and I suppose it's not good, but I guess I'm making up for all the lost years. You know my ex used to make appointments to have sex and write it in his diary."

"Mostly Friday nights after the news and before his favorite sports program. If we were late getting it on, he would turn on the TV whilst we were on it. Nothing like hearing your man cheer on his football team whilst he is pumping away on top of you." Katie blushing, "so you're making up for it now I suppose with that muscle-bound knuckle head your with."

Alice flicks Katie on the bum with a tea towel. "Absolutely! nothing like a good ride after work you should see the size of ....trailing off. Katie puts her fingers on Alice's mouth. "Stop! that's too much information for this time of day." Meanwhile Jeremy has wandered over after putting out the lunch menus and putting on the warming oven. "What am I missing girls, sounds like an interesting conversation, whose riding who?"

Katie ignores Jeremy's intrusion. "Alice, how many times do I have to tell you all I want is a proper relationship not just sex." Jeremy is quick to counter. "You can have both sweetie but trust me, a good man is hard to find but a hard man is good to find, winks and struts away." "Can I have that one Jeremy" says Alice. "Be my guest Alice, just remember where you heard it first when I'm a big film star."

Alice flicks her hair back and looks directly at Katie. "Alright I see your point, but time is ticking girlfriend." Pointing to Katies well-endowed bosom, "won't be long before those two-stop looking pert and turn into spaniel ears, then your options will diminish trust me. Listen, my boyfriend has a buddy. He's a hotty girlfriend! I can line you up if you like but we might need to do something with that hair and makeup." Says Alice fiddling annoyingly with Katies hair and cheek.

Katie brushes Alice's hand away. "Thanks, but no thanks Alice, I'm fine as I am, and I wish I had smaller boobs anyway." Alice with her eyes raised waves her tea towel as she walks away. "Okay but you don't know what you're missing girlfriend. Hey, smiling lewdly, we could even have a threesome with Brad if you like. I think he fancies you and I'm happy to share." Laughing as she goes. Katie throws a dish cloth at Alice. "You never give up do you. I'm not that kind of girl" waving her hand in a dismissive gesture.

Jeremy chips in. "Alice is there any chance he's Bi? Nigel and I might be interested, big you say??" The little trio laughs as Alice heads to the bathroom. Nigel has arrived for the lunchtime rush and is setting about getting his food service area ready. "What did I miss, what's so funny guys?

"Oh, it's nothing really Nigel" says Jeremy putting an arm around Nigel's shoulder. "We were just lining up a threesome with a well-endowed friend of Alice's." Nigel looks up at Jeremy. "You're kidding right?

"Well, yes and no Nige. Says Jeremy winking at Katie, "I know it's your birthday soon and I wanted to get you something big, but your favorite toy shop is out of those rubber things you like." Katie laughs as Nigel chases Jeremy around the café.

CHAPTER 3

STOREROOM LAP DANCER

The day finished, it's time to closeup the café. Everyone has gone except Grumbles and Alice who's turn it is to closeup. Having closed the door and said good night to Grumbles who was in the back storeroom, she is heading to her car a block away when she remembers she left her bag with her keys in it in the storeroom after lunch and heads back to the café to retrieve it before she heads home.

As she heads toward the back of the café, she hears a female voice and giggling as well as Grumbles grunting and cajoling coming from the storeroom. Come on Baby, feed me a cookie, feed me a cookie.

Alice realizes she has caught the boss up to his old tricks. They always knew he was a kinky old bastard, after Katie walked in on him masturbating whilst watching porn, but no one had ever caught him at this stuff before. Alice thinks she might just turn this to her advantage, quietly sneaks into the Café, and quietly turns the security camera toward the action in the stockroom using the remote control under the counter. She makes sure there's a tape running and to be on the safe side she turns on the camera on her cellphone.

Entering the storeroom, she catches Grumbles sitting on a chair half naked with his trouser around his ankles as young semi-nude woman with strategically placed special Cookies gyrates around in front of him, pausing occasionally so he can eat a special Cookies off her body and reveal more of herself, the ritual continues.

Alice casually enters the debauched scene. "Hi Mona, how's it going, hope he pays well." Mona looking non plussed keeps gyrating responds. "Oh, Hi Alice, yes not bad. We call him the cookie monster." Alice holding up a half empty packet of Grumbles special biscuits. "I can see why" she says.

Grumbles starts yelling, "get out, get out the pair of you as he struggles to pull up his pants and hide his pathetic male equipment."

Alice is not missing a beat. "See you for coffee in the morning Mona" who was busy pulling on her dress, Mona smiles, "Sure thing Alice, wouldn't miss it for anything. You might bring the girls with me as well. Same time next week Grumbles"? Grumbles is beside himself and still struggling with his clothing.

"No, you won't! You're all banned, I won't have prostitutes and pimps in my Café, now get out, get out both of you." Strange says Mona looking back as she zips up her dress. "Aren't you on the Town council? You should be familiar with prostitutes and pimps by now." She waves and heads out the door.

Moving closer to Grumbles with a sexy swagger Alice pushes him back on his chair. "So, you like the young ones eh! Well maybe it's time you looked at older women." Grumbles begin to leer and open his mouth to say something; Alice shuts him down. "You know Mona is underage of course." Grumbles stumbles with his words. "What, no she told me she was 21."

Shut up, Grumbles, Alice's face is close to his now. "Your dirty little secret is safe with me. All I need from you is to sign leave requests for Katie and me to attend the Barista contest and approve a pay rise of say 40% for all of us."

Grumbles is panting and sweating profusely. "I'm not approving any leave forms for you two, and your certainly not getting a pay rise." Still fumbling with his pants and shirt he doesn't see Alice pull the tape out of the Security CCTV player and turn the camera back towards the cafe where it originally was.

Waving the tape in her hand as she departs, Alice says. "Oh, I think you will my friend. In fact, I'm sure you will. And lay off us about those crappy Cookies you know you get them to free and it looks like they are part of your afterhours follies also." Grumbles still fumbling with clothing as Alice turns off all the café lights as she leaves.

"Goddam you Alice," he exclaims as he falls on top of recently delivered box of special Cookies, still half dressed. "Goddam you bitch, Ill sack the lot of you, just you wait and see." More crashing sounds.

Yelling over her shoulder Alice Laughs. "Be careful in there Grumbles. You don't want to ruin the special cookies." Strolling out into the alley she catches up with Mona. "Come by in the morning for breakfast. it's on the house. I don't think Grumbles will complain. Hey, bring your girlfriends too. I'd love to see his face when you all walk in. Hope he wasn't rough with you."

Mona smiles. "No, he just likes to look and play with his Cookies if you know what I mean the dirty old bugger." They laugh. Alice points to her car. "Need a lift," Mona? Mona shakes her head. "No thanks Alice, I've got another trick to get to and my bikes the best transport," pointing to a Harley in the lane way.

The next day the Café has a full house of ladies of the night enjoying a free breakfast and chatting with each other as Grumbles walks in. Grumbles stopped in his tracks. What the hell is going on here!!

The Ladies of the night Chorus, all smiling nicely. "Good morning, Cookie, Monster." Other patrons turn and wonder what that's all about. Mona announces to the Café. "He likes special cookies served in a special way, don't you sweetie."

She shakes her booty and smiles as Grumbles heads for the stockroom as fast as he can. The rest of the customers smile and cheers Mona on.

He glares at Alice as he passes. "This is all your doing you evil bitch. You're fired, get out, get out."

Mona comes over and cuddles Grumbles. "Thanks for the wonderful evening last night cheeky boy. Loved the Cookies." Mona pops one down her exposed cleavage and asks, want to taste? She holds up a couple of photos taken from Alice's camera. "They are just as good as last night sweetie."

Grumbles makes a grab for the photos, but she is too quick. "Not so fast cheeky, Cookie first," extracting it from her cleavage and popping it in Grumbles mouth as she turns away. "And thanks for breakfast. Most generous big boy, shall we make it a regular date for breakfast, say once a week for all the girls." flicking her hair, she strolls away as the customer's cheer.

Grumbles spits the Cookie out and turns to Alice. "You still here. I told you you're fired and you might as well take that friend of yours with you too," pointing to Katie.

Alice has a smug look on her face as she looks at Grumbles across the counter. The Café is deadly quiet. "Well, now folks we know why he calls them special Cookies don't we, winks at Katie and the Café bursts into laughter." Grumbles begins waving his hands about and motioning toward the door. "Get out, get out the pair of you and don't come back!"

Alice motions toward Katie with a sweet look on her face. "You know, that's the nicest thing he ever said to me." Turning to Grumbles she announces, "Katie and I will have the day off and see you tomorrow. By the way I will need those leave forms signed by tomorrow and I'll keep this CD from the TV CCTV in case you change your mind somewhere down the line when we need another pay rise."

"On second thoughts, I should send a copy of this to your home. A questioning look crosses her face, "might make good viewing for the family or perhaps the next lodge meeting maybe?"

Grumbles is red with rage. "Bitch, I'll get you for this."

Grabbing her handbag and Katies Arm Alice announces to the customers. Sorry folks, we are off but Grumbles here has offered everyone free coffee today. Come on kiddo we are going shopping.

The ladies of the night all descend on the counter with multiple orders. Jeremy, politely ignoring Grumbles says,

"More coffee and Cookies ladies." Grumbles heads for the storeroom in a state of distress knowing he has been outsmarted and lost control.

CHAPTER 4

A TICKET TO KEEP

E arly next morning Alice is driving her rundown little car to work Windows down, singing along with the music as she usually does, blue and red lights flashing behind catch her attention. Shit, that's all I need now! She mutters to herself. A motorcycle cop behind her is pointing at her to pull over.

Alice curses her luck and wonders what she did wrong this time. Damn, damn, damn. Just what I don't need right now. She fumbles in her worn-out bag beside her with final notice bills sticking out. The motorcycle cop walks up to the driver's window. "License and registration please Maam."

Alice smiles politely and hands over her documents. Sorry officer, what did I do? The Cop accepts the documents. "Thank you Maam. looks at them and looks back at Alice. Say, aren't you the lady from the coffee shop? What's it called again." Sensing a softening Alice fills in the query. "It's the Coffee Stopz over on Alfred Street."

Alice notices the Cops chiseled good looks and strong arms and decides a little flirting might help her situation. Pointing to the name and logo on her nicely filled T-shirt and improving his view of her cleavage, she says. "I see you can read the name on my T-shirt." Cop smiles warmly. "Maam, you make the best coffee in town. I'm a big fan of your Coffee. But those Cookies, they're something else. Does anybody eat those nasty things?"

Alice is tired of the conversation and not wanting to be late says. "Okay just give me the ticket, I'm late." The cop has removed his sunglasses and helmet. Alice notices he is quite handsome and strong-looking and thinks a little flirting might shorten the expense of a ticket that she can ill afford. Batting her eyes and leaning forward so the Cop gets a better view of her assets. "Officer, I was thinking, we could work something out. Coffee maybe" She smiles temptingly. "By the way call me Alice."

Cop smiling broadly puts on his sunglasses. "I know your name Alice; I've just read your license and Rego. I just wanted to tell you your taillight is out, but a cup of your coffee would be good. I'm due for a break soon, I'll drop by and take you up on your offer." He winks and turns to walk back toward his motorcycle.

Alice, warming to the cop, "you do that officer" and smiles over the top of her sunglasses. "I'm sure you'll be satisfied with my service," winking as he puts on his helmet. What's your name? Cop stops and looks straight at Alice. "The names Ben Maam." Alice, smiling broadly, now feels she may have met a bed mate. "Hi Ben, please call me Alice, I know, its sounds like an old lady tag but that's what I was christened."

Ben leaning on the door of the car and taking in the view. "Alice it is and that's a nice name for a nice lady. You have a good day now and don't forget to get that taillight fixed, OK" as he looks over the top of his sunglasses.

The morning rush is over at the café. Alice and Katie are working on the machines and cleaning up as they do the final coffees for a bunch of late starting office workers sitting in the corner discussing their bosses.

Alice takes a breather as she passes over the tray of coffees to Jeremy and busies herself cleaning the dispensing area and filters on the ageing machines.

"I nearly got booked this morning Katie. However, the cop was a hunk, tells me he comes here for Coffee often. I think it was just a come-on line though." Katie motions with her eyes toward the door. "You mean that cop walking in the door and waving." Alice looking flustered. "Geez yes that's him how's my makeup and my hair."

Katie nonchalantly looks away. "Same as usual Alice, too much makeup and too little hair."

Alice glares back at Katie from under the counter as she tries to sort herself out. "Gee thanks Pal."

Katie looking down at Alice fumbling around under the counter. "Better hurry Alice he is here and smiling. seems nice, big one too, just you're type."

Alice stops what she's doing. "Keep your eyes off him kiddo, he's mine, anyway, he is too old for you."

Ben arrives at the counter and smiles at Katie. "Is Alice here? She promised me a special coffee and cookie."

Alice peering sheepishly over the top of the counter notices Ben smiling down at her. "Oh! Hi, Ben, just looking for those Cookies you love." She pretends to be fumbling under the counter.

Katie notices that Alice has made a mess of her lipstick and jumps in front of her. "Coffee officer"

Holding out his hand, "Names Ben, I'm not on duty now." Katie smiles and nods. "As you wish Ben, I'm sure Alice will be with you soon as she finds what she is looking for under the counter." Kicks Alice gently. Alice is still fumbling under the counter and after Katies kick she falls over and up ends herself with her dress and apron up around her waist. "Be right with you Ben. I'll be right there."

Ben moves quickly around the counter and lifts her off the floor with his strong arms. Their eyes meet, and he holds her a little too long until, embarrassed, they separate. "Are you Ok," he says, looking into her eyes?

"I am now, thanks Ben." smiling lovingly back at the handsome cop holding her arm. "Coffee is coming and here's your special Cookie" she says holding out a broken cookie.

Taking the cookie and smiling Ben says, "flat white no sugar please Katie." Still standing too close and still holding her arm Ben says, "hold the Cookies, I've already cleaned the tires on the bike." Smiling he releases his gently grip on her arm whilst dusting her down. They both giggle like school kids. "Go grab a seat Ben and I'll bring it over."

Ben moves off toward a vacant table at the back of the café. "Can you come join me when you have a break? I've got some paperwork to do but it should be done in a few minutes" he asks. Alice still flushed and fumbling makes a mess of the brew Katie has made for Ben. "Damn I'm all fingers and thumbs today."

Having already made his coffee once Katie starts another one and hands the finished coffee to Alice. "Here take his coffee and get over their before he and it go cold. It's your break time anyway so go get him girlfriend." She pushes Alice towards the opening in the counter. "Go on git!"

Time marches on and Alice is happily talking to Ben. Both are smiling and the chemistry looks good from where Katie is standing. Grumbles emerges from his endless stock take and piles of dirty magazines he thinks no one knows about and interrupts the pair, chastising Alice. Why aren't you behind the counter? I'm not paying you good money to socialize with the customers.

Ben stands up and his imposing frame gets in Grumbles face. In a nice tone and with a smile on his face that intimidates Grumbles, Ben explains that he had a few questions about the health and safety and food safety permits for the place. Knowing he was snookered and a little afraid of Ben he backs away. "That's Ok then, carry on. If you have any further questions I'll be in the back."

Ben holds up his hand. One question please sir. "Is that your Volvo parked out front?"

Grumbles hesitates as he answers. "Yes officer, that's my car why? Bn pauses "Sir, your parked in a two-hour zone and your left front tyre is badly worn. I'd get that seen to asap." Ben reaches into his pocket for his infringement book. Tapping it with his pen.

Grumbles gets the message. "I will do it straight away Officer. Thanks for pointing it out." He hurries out of the café and heads to his car. Ben smiles at Alice. Shall we have dinner Saturday night Maam? She nods agreement as he hands her a note written on a napkin and heads out the door. "Pick you up at your place 7 o'clock, right?" Alice without hesitating. "OK, Ben but what should I wear"? Ben stops at the door. "Whatever you decide will look good on you." He winks and walks out the door. The Sound of a motorcycle starting up in the background raises Katies attention from behind the counter.

As Alice returns to the counter, Katie is curious. "So, what was all that about?" Alice looking non-plussed. "Oh nothing, just Grumbles being Grumbles." Katie with eyebrows raised, and pointing to the note Alice was clutching. Looking casual whilst she fusses behind the counter Alice says. "No big deal really. He asked me to go to dinner on Saturday night, that's all."

Stopping what she is doing Katie remonstrates with Alice. "That's all! That's all. I'd say that's a hot date you've got grandma."

"Enough with the grandma stuff right, pointing a finger at Katie, says Alice, "I guess he is alright," slight smile on her face. Turning to Katie and looking non plussed she says, "I might go." Katie is quick to jump on that myth. "Rubbish, you're going, I know you are." The pair squeal and cuddle as girls do from time to time when they are excited. Jeremy joins in having heard the conversation and the invitation first-hand.

One problem Alice, says Jeremy, "what about your current boyfriend?" Alice waves her hands in the air. "Oh him! he left me last week for some body building female. They can flex their muscles together for all I care." Katie frowning, "I thought you two were serious.?"

"Not really Katie, I couldn't stand competing for the Mirror and all his weird foodstuff clogging up my cupboards. Sex was good though. Would you believe he could hold an erection for..."

Katie cuts her short, "enough, enough! I really don't want all the details thank you."

Katie says Alice "I've got an idea. How about a double date Saturday night?"

"No way Alice, I'm not fond of men in uniform."

"Okay" says Alice, "what about we get you hooked up with one of those young trendy types that come here for their Lattes and stuff. Even a lawyer. See that bunch over there" Alice nods toward a group of young men sitting in the corner." What about I set you up with one of them? They are mostly lawyers from what I've heard of their conversations."

"Are you sure Alice? I mean it would be nice to have a date with an educated man, but would they want to go out with a coffee girl."

"Katie the last time they were in I overheard them talking about legal stuff and prosecutors' stuff. Ben knew them this morning as well, so I figured they must all be lawyers."

" OK Alice, but what would a wealthy, young, lawyer want with a worn-out Coffee maker like me?"

"Katie girl, you need a tidy up and a makeover and you'll be a real winner leave the lawyer thing to me. I'll line one up for you."

Jeremy listening to the discussion chips in.

"Makeover sounds like a job from Nigel and I. Leave it to us girlfriend. We know how to do that stuff don't we sweetie" gives Nigel a peck on the cheek.

Saturday morning sees Jeremy, Nigel and Katie going in and out of shops trying on clothes, getting her hair and nails done and make-up fixed.

Later in the day back in Alice place, Nigel, Jeremy, and Alice's daughter Kim are all fussing around Katie. Alice comes in from her shopping trip and stops in her tracks.

"Wow! Where's that mousy little girl gone? You look fabulous kiddo." Jeremy and Nigel, turn Katie around on the swivel chair, "see sweetie told you we could do it." Jeremy with his head close to Katies. They all high-five, a

Ok Alice says Nigel "all she needs now is the date you promised her."

"All sorted team. I've lined up a lawyer who will be your date tonight and I believe he is a prosecutor," says Alice.

Katie got out of her chair cautiously to not disturb the work done on her.

"That's good Alice but I've never met the guy. How do you know he'll like me? Is he cute? Has he seen me, which one was he??"

"Stop, stop Katie! He's a Lawyer, a Prosecutor, what more could you want. Yes, he saw you around the Café, but I showed him a photo from your high school yearbook which he liked."

"You did what Alice! That was taken years ago, and I had braces and plats in those days, tell me you didn't show him that one surely."

Waving her objections away and pointing at her. "Think of it this way kiddo, he is going to get a pleasant surprise if he remembers the photo, I showed him and the way you look in the café compared to now, you're a knockout babe."

"Thanks for that compliment, I think, so what arrangements did you make with him?"

"All under control kiddo, in about half an hour we are meeting the guys at the cafe. I've got to throw on some war paint and get dressed. Can you drop us off Jeremy."

"Certainly sweetie," says Jeremy nodding to Katie, "you look fabulous girlfriend. Come on Kim, says Nigel, it's your turn to look fabulous." Grabs Kim's arm and they stride off to Kim's bedroom with trays of makeup and hair product.

Katie with an indignant look on her face and hands on hips stops at Alice's Bedroom door. "The café Alice, you're kidding right? We're not going there to eat surely."

Appearing from the bathroom with hairbrush in her hand Alice explains. "Don't worry we won't be staying it's just a kick-off point. Ben suggested we go to Ameche's for dinner then I'm bringing him back here, so he can show me his police truncheon and self-defense moves if you know what I mean."

Both giggling like naughty schoolgirls Katie stops the merriment "Alice you never ever stop do you. What about Kim." Alice smiling benignly says to Katie, "she'll be fine with Jeremy and Nigel tonight at their place. Besides, since mighty mouse left and took his sword, I've not been getting any so I'm overdue for a romp or two."

CHAPTER 5

---◄●►---

KATIE'S BLIND DATE

I ts early evening and the pre-movie set are dropping in for coffee and a snack at the café. Grumbles and his wife are fumbling with the orders and yelling at each other.

"I don't know how you get the ladies to make coffee with these damn things John." Snapping back "Just get on with it you know I can't afford new machines and penalty rates for a Saturday night" says grumbles to his wife as they struggle with the ancient equipment.

Alice and Katie are dropped off at the café by Jeremy. They walk into the café and Grumbles stopped what he was doing with his mouth open. "Close your mouth John, it's just your two Baristas," says his wife. "I'll get their order you just wrestle that thing into action and stop gawking."

Brad the delivery man drops in for a coffee on his way to the movies with a date. Seeing Katie and Alice all dressed up in their finery he comes over. Alice has seen Ben pull up and is off to greet him at the door leaving Brad and his date to talk to Katie.

"You look gorgeous Katie, what's the big occasion"? Answering nonchalantly, "Oh nothing much, just a date."

"That's nice with whom may I ask says Brad"?

"Oh, just a boy friend of mine, you probably won't know him, he's a lawyer." Brads is getting anxious and a little jealous. "Brad darling, I think we need to go if we are going to make the movie." "Ok, but we have time Sarah. Oh, sorry, Katie, this is Sarah."

"Nice to meet you Katie but we really must go Brad" says Sarah pulling at Brads sleeve as she notices him admiring Katie. "Katie, I didn't think you had a boyfriend from the way you spoke."

"Of course, I do Brad," she notices Alice waving from the door. "I've always had a boyfriend, in fact here he comes now." A short plump bespectacled man in crumpled clothing approaches Katies table.

Smiling at himself Brad allows himself to be dragged away by the increasingly desperate Sarah. "OK, have a nice evening, Katie."

The short fat man is looking Katie up and down, blows his nose and holds out his hand. "Hi, my names Bernard but friends all call me Bern. You scrubbed up well for a coffee maid"? Still looking her up and down whilst holding her hand.

Holding his clammy hand Katie is surprised by a BO laden embrace from Bern. She makes a scowling face at Alice over his shoulder. Alice shrugs her shoulders. "Nice to meet you Bern.

Grumbles came over to their table. "You lot going to order anything or just occupy my tables."

Alice arrives at the table with Ben in tow. "Evening Grumbles, we will have 4 full premium flat whites thank you cafe owner and don't forget those special Cookies", winks at Katie and Ben

Grumbles heads back to the counter muttering to himself about rude people and the abbreviation of his name.

After their stop at the Café, they head off to an upmarket restaurant in Ben's car. Katie is stuck with Bern in the back, who smells like a wet sheep dog. The restaurant is sumptuous, and a string trio is playing in the corner. Soup had not long

been served and Bernard (Bern)has taken to drinking directly from the bowl to the amazement of everyone in the place. To diffuse the increasingly embarrassing situation Ben asks, "Bernard I believe you're a lawyer? Can't say I've noticed you around the courthouse?"

Bernard is busy slurping his soup looks up.

"Please call me Bern," with soup on his chin and down the napkin tucked into his shirt front he looks at the trio opposite him.

"Good God no, who told you that? I'm a filing clerk at city hall. Dad got me the job, it's great. I get time to myself as the other clerks seem to want to do all the work."

Katie is fuming under a fake smile and shoots disparaging looks across the table at Alice. Ben notices the growing tension between the ladies and tries to find some middle ground for discussion. "I'm, sorry Bern I thought someone said you were a prosecutor."

"Oh that, yes, I am that. I'm a prosecutor in the online video game called Justice. I've risen to the fifth rank in that area and I'm proud of having done that. Do you know the game?" Ben, looking a little jaded,

"Not really Bern, I'm a cop and my spare time is spent horse riding and hiking. The last thing I want to see is more court room stuff,"

Bernard cutting off Alice who was about to say something spits bread sticks as he hurriedly speaks. "that's amazing I love horses and animals too in fact I have a cool hobby that might interest you guys."

Wondering what on earth they may have in common, Ben asks, "Oh-really, do you ride. "

Bernard still devouring all the breadsticks waves a half chewed one at Ben.

"Good God no Ben! My hobby is making clothing out of dog and cat hair." Alice and Katie cough part of their soup up and gag at the thought. Ben is sitting open mouthed. Not to be put off Bern continues excitedly,

"Yes, it's a great hobby I get the hair from the animal shelter. With that he stands up and turns around knocking a glass of wine over Katie. See this jacket it's almost pure Alsatian with a little bit tabby for the collar."

Katie is glaring at Alice across the table. "I need the bathroom; I think I'm going to be sick. COMING Alice!"

In the lady's bathroom Katie is trying to get stains out of her new dress and is sobbing. Her makeup has run.

"I should have known you would set me up with, with, with that thing out there." Tears rolling down her cheeks. "I thought you were my friend."

Trying to apologize Alice goes to put an arm around Katie. "I'm sorry Katie I thought he was a prosecutor the way he was talking with his friends at the time."

"You idiot that was his video gaming group that comes in the cafe regularly, never again okay. I'll get my own date next time and you're taking me home right now." Taken aback by the forthright outburst from the normally meek Katie, Alice tries to reason with her.

"What about my night with Ben and his truncheon?"

"I don't care about your night Alice, mine and my dress are ruined. You can play hide the Truncheon with him another time just get me out of here from goodness' sake. I've never been so embarrassed and just look at my dress, its completely ruined and I'm paying it off."

A little later Alice and Katie are driven home in Ben's car. Ben tries to break the icy silence.

"Interesting guy your boyfriend Katie."

With venom in her voice Katie responds. "He is not my boyfriend it was Alice's idea of an ideal blind date."

Taken aback a little Ben apologizes. "I'm sorry Katie, I really didn't know. The little shit stuck me for the bill after telling me he had overspent on his latest addition to his beer can collection. What a loser."

Alice trying to save the awkward situation and her first date with Ben.

"I'm sorry about that Ben, I'll pay our half of the bill, it's my fault she had the date from hell. How is the little creep getting home?"

"To be honest Alice, I hope the Animal welfare mob pick him up as a stray." The tense mood is broken, and the trio laugh about the whole sorry affair as the car disappears into the night.

CHAPTER 6

---◄○►---

NERDY FRIENDS

A day later Alice and Katie are busy at their coffee machines. Neither has spoken to each other much and Katie is holding her resentment. Alice is keen to patch things up with her friend and decides to jump right in.

"Katie, I'm so sorry about the other night. I really thought he was a lawyer and a prosecutor."

With a friendly look at her long-time friend Katie, she soothes the situation. "It's okay I forgive you but don't do it again alright."

Alice makes a Boy Scout sign. "I promise Kiddo, no more blind dates. However, I think you might have missed out on a dog hair jacket with a pussy cat collar." Katie smiles knowingly and softly punches Alice in the arm.

"Not my taste Alice but your welcome to accept the option. Look who has just walked in." Katie says.

Looking toward the door Alice sees the regular group of gamers enter the cafe with Bernard at the back looking very sheepish. They head to the far table whispering and sniggering to each other. Jeremy returning with their coffee orders whispers to Katie.

"Is that the nerd you went out with the other night?"

"Yes, unfortunately," she replies, noticing the giggling going on at the nerd's table. "What are they so happy about?"

Jeremy looks toward the wall and whispers to Katie and Alice. "They're saying you slept with Bernard and they're drawing straws to see who hits on your next. They reckon you're easy meat."

Holding the normally placid Katie back from going over the table Alice says. "Leave this to me sweetie and struts over to the sniggering group in the corner. Striking in a provocative pose, she says.

"Hello boys what's your pleasure. I hear your drawing straws from a night out with Katie" bending forward and leaning on their table she exposes her ample cleavage. Knowing she has their full attention she goes ahead to layout an offer.

"Tell you what guys, I reckon Katie and I could take you all on out the back. Once you've had your coffee of course." She pauses with a sexy smile on her face stirring one of their cups with a finger and then putting it in her mouth slowly. "Yuck, not enough sugar. You're going to need your strength to keep up with us boys." The group of nerds is speechless and highly excited.

"Tell you what boys, I think you need some of our special coffee for the job in hand. On the house of course. I'll bring it to you personally then when you're done, we will meet you in the back alley. That is of course if you're up to it."

Alice turns as she walks away, hips swinging. Turning back toward the gibbering bunch of nerds she caps off their excitement. "Oh! and remember guys, bring your best game as we are hard to satisfy, aren't we Bern" She winks at him knowingly. The other nerds turn to him and begin interrogating him.

The nerds are beside themselves with excitement. Bernard is still sheepish but has become the hero of the day and recognized as the nerdy stud muffin of the moment. Knowing the truth has not stopped Bern from conjuring up the pleasures that await them and expands on his story and conquests to outlandish levels as Alice expected.

Meantime, Alice has returned to the counter where the nerd's Coffee order has been prepared. Reaching under the counter and right to the back Alice pulls out two small tins of powder and sprinkles a little powder from each tin into the coffees. Thinks for a moment and empties most of both tins into the coffees.

"What on earth are you doing Alice" says Katie seeing her fiddling with the coffee order.

"Just follow my lead kiddo and go along with whatever I say, trust me, I'm going to fix that little bastard and his nerdy mates." Heading back to the nerd's table with Katie behind her Alice places the coffees on the table, bending forward close to each one of the nerds giving them a nice view of her ample cleavage.

"Here you go guys, special coffee." Alice smiles sexily, licking her lips she says. This will put lead in your pencil," winks and struts away, hips swinging.

"Meet us in the alley in 15 min, and make sure you're ready for action." Alice and Katie make a suggestive gesture in their direction as they walk back to the counter.

Whispering to Alice once back behind the counter Katie says. "What on earth are you doing. I'm not going out in the alley with that bunch of misfit perverts." Alice puts her hand on Katies shoulder. "Trust me kiddo, this is going to be fun."

Katie is not so sure and expresses her concerns. "Alice, you know Grumbles is away today and there's just Jeremy here. What if they turn violent and demanding? I don't want to get raped and beaten up by those guys."

Ducking into the storeroom with Katie in tow Alice calms Katie down. "Don't worry honey, I've got it sorted. Just let me know when they start making a move towards the back alleyway." The nerds seem a little disoriented as they head out the side door to the blind alley behind the Café smiling lewdly at the two women. Alice gets the nod from Katie and gets on her mobile phone.

"Ben, sorry to trouble you at work honey but we have a little situation at the cafe. There is a bunch of weirdos in the alley behind the cafe I think they're on drugs and their exposing themselves and other things." Theres a pause as Ben gets his colleagues organised. Alice smiles at Katie as she goes back into the café with her phone still in her ear.

"Okay thanks Ben. we will lock all the doors and make sure they can't get in." as she signals to Jeremy and Katie to do so. Alice runs over to the bags the nerds left on their table expecting to return triumphant. She sprinkles a little of the powder from one of the near empty tins on each of the bags and wiping the tin clean of her prints, puts the empty tin into Bernards bag.

"That'll fix his wagon" she says to Katie and Jeremy

In the back alley the group of nerds are swaying around, disoriented and most have their pants down around their ankles, one guy is being sick whilst others have defecated. Some are clutching their tummies which shows that they may be next to follow. Meanwhile Alice, Katie and Jeremy have locked the back and front doors and put up a closed sign. The nerds stumbling about start banging on the back door pleading to be let in.

A police cruiser pulls up blocking the gated end of the alley. The nerds are struggling to pull up their pants at the sight of the approaching police officers.

"What sort of weirdos have we here Bill"

"Not sure but I think we might need the fire brigade to hose them down. Gawd the smell" Holding their noses as they approach the staggering, defecating bunch of nerds.

"I'll grab that service hose and wash them down before we stick them in the van." Says the lead cop The nerds are beginning to collapse in their own mess and still have not got their pants pulled up. A sergeant turns up and surveys the scene.

"What the hell have we got here Bill."

"The Café ladies called to say they were being threatened by a bunch of men exposing themselves in the service alley behind the Café. This is what we found when we got here. I think they're high on something and as you can see some have erections and most have shit themselves."

"Geez, Bill. That's the mayor's son Bernard, isn't it and that looks like councilor Johnson's son also. I'll get backup but they will need to go to hospital for testing. Where are the ladies that reported it"

"They're Inside Sarge. We told them to lock themselves in."

The police sergeant is let into the café and the story is revealed. Jeremy is the first to speak. "Well, officer, I heard them talking about sexual things in relation to Katie here. I asked them to be a bit more respectful and they told me piss off." Alice then gives her story. "As Mr. Grumbelton is away today, I'm in charge of the café. When Jeremy told me what he had heard, I went over and asked them to leave once they had finished their coffee.

The Sargent is busy taking notes. "So how did they wind up in the service alley."

"They continued making rude and disparaging comments about Katie and they said they would like to, as well you know, have their way with both of us." Sargent looks up from his notes. "You mean they threatened to rape you." Well yes Sarge, they said they were going to do us in the service alley."

Sarge continues writing. "So, what happened then Miss."

Alice looking distressed. "Well, the small fat one ushered them out into the alley to setup the scene, the old mattress the homeless guy sometimes uses, I don't know. Anyway, he said they would be back and for us to get ready for it or something to that effect. I told Katie and Jeremy to lock all the doors after I rang you and spoke with Ben, we've been dating recently" she explains.

"I see says the sergeant. You did the wise thing. There has been a group of rapists running around the town lately and this might just be them. Do you know any of them other than here as customers" Alice looks at Katie. "Sarge, I had a blind date with Bernard, but it was just dinner and that was a disaster."

"I see" says the sergeant. "Can you give me details of the date?"

"It was a double date with Ben Sarge. We went to Ameche's restaurant, but we left Bernard there as his manners and attitude were appalling.

"Ok, Ill check with Ben back at the station but do you think Bernard might have been led to believe there was more to the date Miss."

Katie thinks for a moment. "It's possible I suppose but I certainly left him in no doubt about my revulsion of him after he spilled wine all over my new dress and spoke about his dog hair clothing hobby."

"Thank you, Miss, clearly, he is a fruitcake. Did they leave anything here in the café" Alice points to the bags around the table the nerds were sitting at. "Those are theirs." She goes to pick them up. The Sergeant stops her, "don't touch Maam! We suspect they are on drugs and they may be carrying them in their bags. I'll have an officer bag them up. Meantime if you ladies need any help or counseling, don't hesitate to call this number."

Brad, the delivery guy, arrives as the nerds are being shuffled into a police van. He knocks on the front door wondering why they are closed and what all the police presence is about. The ladies let him in. "What the hell is going on out their ladies, what's with all the cops and fire hose stuff."

Alice has a slight smile on her face as she explains. "That's a gang of perverts who the police suspect of sex offences in the area. They think we were a target after Katie had a double date with that fat little one called Bernard.

Brad looking shocked. "Really, that's a bit close to home for you ladies. How did they catch them" Katie now warming to the lie explains.

"Appears someone saw them cavorting in the alley with their pants down and called the Cops." Alice looking serious. "They had just left here after Coffee would you believe. High as kites, the officer told us. We were lucky they didn't assault us what with Grumbles not being here today. We were lucky I think."

Leaning on the counter he sees the Barista competition brochure poking out of Alices apron. "What's that? are you ladies thinking of entering the competition."

"We were but Grumbles won't let us practice our routines on his machines even though he gave us leave and we promised to do our practice after hours," says Alice.

Brad holds up a hand. "Hey, you know what, I can try and have a word with my boss, he might even be interested in sponsoring you two. Let me talk to the boss and see if I can get you both an interview."

"That would be great Brad, we don't have much time though Do you have the machines they use in the competition? asks Alice.

"We certainly do Alice. We have all the latest models in our test area and I guess that's where you could practice. Who knows we might even learn something from you two as well?

After things have settled down, Katie turns to Alice and quietly asks.

"What the fuck was in those brews."

Turning to Katie with a naughty glint in her eye she says

"Do you really want to know kiddo. Wait, don't answer that as then you could be a coconspirator."

Looking at Alice quizzically,

"I thought that was a given anyway, so fess up so I can at least know what I'm going to prison for."

"OK kiddo, this goes no further than between us and I'm getting rid of the evidence straight after this chat, The coffee is my regular Columbian grind but it has some opioids ground in courtesy of Mr. Muscles that I was dating at the time. He liked to drink coffee with a punch. I always made myself scarce when he made this stuff. It also had some erectile stuff in it and he would stay erect for hours and high as a kite to boot.

"The kick in it was my addition of a very powerful laxative mix that I was prescribed during a stay in hospital. I added that to try and get rid of him but he seemed to like being high, erect, and shitting himself. He called it his surge and purge ritual. I only hope he kept some to use with his new girlfriend."

"Bloody hell Alice, that could kill someone, was it wise to use it on those idiots."

Winking at Katie as she bags up the tins and wipes down the shelf with a strong bleach mixture. "It worked didn't it."

"Remind me not to get on the wrong side of you "

Putting her arm around Katies shoulder they head out to the incinerator to dispose of the evidence.

"This way matter Hari junior"

They giggle as they dispose of the evidence tipping the containers into the incinerator.

CHAPTER 7

PRACTICE BEGINS

A day later the ladies drive up to an impressive modern building with a large sign up front 'COFFEE HOUSE, The home of coffee excellence.

Alice looking up at the sign and the magnificent building wonders why cheapskate Grumbles could be dealing with the likes of these guys. They're major players in the Coffee business. Walking through the impressive foyer and displays and looking around Katie knows they have arrived in Coffee heaven, checking out the coffee machines Alice was amazed that some of them had not been released yet as she had only seen them mentioned in Barista monthly magazine when Brad dropped off a copy.

Alice turns with a smile on her face.

"I think we will have a good time here kiddo, I wonder if one San Remos over there would fit in my handbag. Or if one of those grinders could fit down your blouse at least we could nick some of those Barista annual magazines over there."

"I'm not that kind of girl Alice. Besides there's no centerfold in those magazines, is there? No wait, I seem to recall they have the coffee pot of the month don't they." Both women giggle like naughty schoolgirls.

Brad walks up behind the ladies in his delivery uniform.

"I see you've found our display area. As you can see, we've got all the latest stuff here ladies. I think the marketing manager wants to see you both. From what I've heard he thinks it's a good idea to sponsor you. Brad points towards a well-dressed older man standing beside the very impressive reception desk area. I think that's him now so good luck I am off to make some more deliveries."

Anxious to get a started Alice heads towards the man at the reception desk. Still standing behind Katie, Brad turns to her nervously and says. "Before you go can I ask you something?"

Turning to meet his eyes Katie pauses. "Sure, what is it?"

"Well, I was wondering, I mean I was thinking umm."

In the distance Alice is beckoning to Katie. Come.

Katie waves to Alice, signals indicating she is coming,

"Sorry Brad, I must go. See you next time you make deliveries." She quietly smiles thinking he is quite cute as she walks away.

Knowing he missed his chance to ask Katie a crucial question, Brad turns and heads away into the building. He walks back to a large office in the corner taking off is work shirt as he goes. An older lady sitting at a desk outside the large office stops him.

Brads secretary Zelda asks, "well how did it go Brad."

The look on Brads face says it all to her. "You didn't ask her, did you."

"Well, no Zelda the timing was wrong, but I'll try again tomorrow when I go the café." Zelda shaking her head. "Brad you are hopeless." With his hands cradling his head Brad shuffles into the large corner office. "I know Zelda, I know."

Down in the bowels of the large complex the ladies are in the test lab at the factory end of the complex. The marketing manager is showing them the Coffee machines that will be used in the competition and explaining the operating details. He hands each of them a personalized apron and an entry card so they can come and go as they please. A room full of stock is pointed out and the marketing manager shakes hands and walks away.

They high-five each other realising they were truly in coffee heaven, as they look at these blends available and swoon over some of the machines and what they I wouldn't give to having one of those babies in Coffee Stopz. Alice cuddles a shiny new machine.

Over the next two weeks the two women spend every spare moment and long into the night practicing their routines and honing their coffee making skills. Initially there are disasters that the ladies laugh at but as the time for them to leave for competition draws near, they become more agitated at the errors which lead to arguments.

On their final night of practice Katie turns to Alice.

"I'm sorry, I know I've been a pain in the butt with all this stuff. I just want to give us the best shot at the contest. I think it's my only way out of this town."

"Don't be silly Katie, I'm just a reactionary bitch and I need the kick in the pants to strive for our success. I know you want to get out of this town and to improve yourself. So do I so let's just relax and give it our best shot and have fun whilst we are at it. What do you say"?

Katie hugs Alice and stands back. "You really are a good friend. Now what about one more run through Grandma." Alice chases her around the test lab. laughing and giggling.

CHAPTER 8

ANOTHER BLIND DATE

A day or so later, at the cafe the ladies are back at their tired old coffee machines as usual. They have put hours and hours into perfecting their blends and styles and putting some work into their special brew if they get the chance to do it for a final place.

Both feel they're as ready as they will ever be and are due to leave in a couple of days to get there in time for the start of the competition. Both have packed their winning dress just in case.

Alice as ever confident turns to Katie as they finish off the last brews for the morning rush "I think we are going to do well if we keep our heads and concentrate on what we are doing and just relax Katie.

Katie has been focused on this opportunity and responds "Concentrating is not a problem for me Alice. You've got a few distractions though with that new boyfriend of yours.

Nodding Alice replies "Okay, point taken Katie. We are thinking of moving in together at his ranch outside town."

"Do tell mystery woman. So, when did all this happen."

Alice moves closer to Katie as she manipulates the coffee machines with practiced skills. "Remember the night when Ben picked us up at the Coffee supply factory? Well, after we dropped you off, he drove me out to his ranch and asked me there. It was a nice surprise and quite unexpected."

"I guess you were impressed with his ranch or was it his truncheon? So, when does the big move happen" says Katie?

Not to be put off Alice opens some phone pictures "Katie, wait till you see his ranch, its beautiful, and I'm looking forward to getting out of that little apartment I'm in. However, we are still thinking about it. Yes, his truncheon is impressive, and he knows how to use it. Years of Police training I suspect." She says grinning naughtily.

They both laugh out loud causing customers to look up and Grumbles to pop his head around the corner. "What's so funny get back to work, you're disturbing the customers."

"Katie don't worry about my love life girlfriend yours is non-existent." Says Alice flicking Katies hair annoyingly.

"I'm okay Alice, I think it's the bachelorette or Nunnery life is for me."

Alice looks skyward making a picture frame with her out-stretched hands. "I can see it now, sister Katie Cappuccino of the order of Espresso." She moves her hands down to frame Katies face. "This is you. Got news for you, not going to happen Kiddo. I'm determined to get you hooked up. You wait and see what I come up with next."

Katie moves closer to Alice. "Oh no you don't sister. Remember the last disaster? I'm still paying off that ruined dress and those nerds are still spreading rumors about us."

"I'm sorry about that little episode Katie, but I fixed their little wagons, didn't I? Besides their reputations are shot and nobody listens to their ravings. Anyway kiddo, you see that table in the corner with three smartly dressed guys in suits. Especially the dark one in the corner." Peering out from behind the Coffee machine Katie catches sight of a tall good-looking guy in the corner looking back and smiling.

Alice whispers to Katie, "hunky or what"

Nodding agreement Katie turns to Alice. Okay, he's a hunk but what's that got to do with anything."

"Katie, girlfriend, he's a banker drives a nice-looking BMW and he wants to take you out tonight, okay?"

Immediately on guard Katie marches Alice into a corner. "Oh no you don't. I thought I said no more fiddling in my love life."

Katie sees Alice gesturing toward the counter with her eyes and turns to find the tall dark young man leaning across the counter.

In a matter of fact voice he says, "Katie, 7 PM I'll pick you up here and I don't like to be late. On second thoughts, make that 7 PM at your place I have the address don't be late like I said." As he turns and walks away with an air of superiority.

Trying to get on the front foot Katie calls after the young man as he walks away. "Hey! pardon me but who are you and how do you know where I live." glaring at Alice who has turned her back and on her and gone sheepish.

"So, what's your name and where exactly are we supposed to be going?"

Banker type, walking away nonchalantly brushes the question away.

"The names Don and wear something nice. 7 PM right! and walks out of the cafe."

Katie is looking for Alice who has snuck out the back. "Where are you Alice, because I am going to kick your butt from here to the moon and back."

Despite misgivings, during the rest of the day Alice and Jeremy persuaded Katie to go on the date and promised to help her get ready. That evening at Katies house, Don in the BMW pulls up and honks the horn.

Alice peering out through the curtains. "Katie, looks like your dates here, but he is not getting out of the car the rude little bastard."

Jeremy puts his hand on Alice's shoulder. "I think that's the way they do it these days Alice.

"So, but not with my Katie he doesn't. The rude little bastard better come introduce himself or I'll go out there and teach him some manners."

Coming down the stairs Katie overhears the conversation. "It's okay guys I'll go out no need to make a fuss." Katie walks down the path to the car and opens the door to jump in.

Don looking at his watch. "You're a little late Katie. I don't like being late."

Trying to fasten her seatbelt as he speeds off, Katie asks. "Sorry we were talking. Anyway, where are we going Don." With an arrogant tone Don responds.

"Never you mind sweetheart it's a classy place you've probably never been to before," as he eyes her up and down in glances whilst driving. "That the best you can do sweety"?

Looking hurt, Katie responds.

"What's wrong with my dress."

"Looks cheap but you fill it out nicely, so it will do, I guess. Says Don as he turns up the radio, stifling any further conversation.

Katie sits back in her seat feeling insulted and wishing she had stood up to Alice and not gone on this damn date. The car pulls up to a swank country club. A car park attendant greets Don as he steps out of his car. Doing his rehearsed meet and greet job he walks up to Don. "Welcome to Pine Lakes Country Club Sir."

Don pushes the car keys into the young lad's chest. "If there is one mark on this car when I get it back, I will tear you another backside, right! I've memorized the mileage so no joyrides."

Leaving the young Car Park attendant shaken and in no doubt, he is dealing with a tosser, he jumps in and is about to drive off and park the car when he notices Katie is still sitting in the car.

Don has walked off towards the entrance to the club. leaving. Katie sat in the passenger seat in the hope that Don was a gentleman and would open the door for her. "Oh! sorry Maam, I thought he was on his own."

Smiling at the young lad she expresses her opinion. "Might as well be, I think I'm just along for the ride." She smiles at the young man as she gets out of the car. "Theres one in every crowd you know. Hope he tips you." She says smiling at the young man.

Entering the club on her own Katie sees Don at the bar with a bunch of his cronies. A snooty voice from behind stops her in her tracks. "I'm sorry madam, its members only and we don't allow unescorted women into the premises."

Katie has had enough and pointing toward Don at the bar says, "I'm with him if you don't mind.

Looking her up and down the doorman responds. "Sorry, that's an old trick Madam you'll have to leave."

Katie is now furious "Not on your nelly buddy. As she pushes past him heading for the group with the Doorman in pursuit.

As she approaches the group she announces her presence loudly, "hey! Hotshot "she pushes Don in the back spilling his drink. "Remember me."

The doorman approaches'- "I'm sorry Mr. Adley, she pushed past me and I couldn't stop her."

Don holding up a hand says "it's okay she is with me" whilst. turning back to the bar to order another drink.

"Bartender, another martini from me and she will have a white wine with a twist."

Pushing in front of Don, Katie is abrupt with her words. "No, she bloody well won't. She will have a beer please."

The bartender smiles politely. Don interrupts the bartender Turning to Katie, he scolds her saying. "No, you won't we are having fish and ladies don't drink beer here sweetheart. Bring her a glass of white wine." The wine arrives and he hands the glass of wine to Katie.

Katie, now at breaking point let's fly. "Oh really, well here is what you can do with your white wine Mr. Adley," tipping it down his trouser front. "Now you listen to me BUCKO, I'm going to sit down and order a steak. I might let you join me but then again, I might not. Either way, you're paying. Right" says! Katie as she stormed off into the dining room leaving Don with wine-soaked trousers and a bunch of his cronies laughing their heads off.

Love what you've done with your Trousers Don. Can't wait to see what you do next. And other comments fly as Don heads to the golfing end of the club to get a pair of dry trousers out of his locker.

Heading towards an empty table with the Maître d' in hot pursuit, she is halfway across the floor when she feels an arm on a shoulder. Thinking it was Don, without turning around she says.

"Listen bucko I've had a bad day, I'm hungry, I need a beer and steak and you're paying right, so back off and go eat someplace else."

Getting ready to punch her assailant she turns around to find Brad has her arm and has waived off the maître d'. Katie is astonished,

"YOU! what are you doing here. This is a bit out of your league, isn't it?" Looking him up and down, she notes how smartly dressed he is and handsome out of his delivery uniform.

Smiling broadly Brad bows slowly "Yes Maam, I'm the delivery guy and I am here to deliver dinner to a beautiful lady." Brad escorts her to his table and pulls out her chair for her. Looking slightly bemused Katie whispers to him as she sits down.

"Listen, this place looks way too expensive for a delivery guys pay packet, we can go Dutch if you like or just order the soup and we can get a burger somewhere."

Smiling fondly, Brad grabs her hand gently. "Don't worry about it. The meals on me."

A waiter arrives to take their orders.

"May I order for you", he asks Katie, she nods, "two beers to start please and I think the lady would like a steak", turning to Katie for the nod of agreement, "and I will have the same, both medium rare, I think" Checks with Katie, who nods approval again. "With all the trimmings please"

As the meal progresses the couple talk and laugh as the night goes on and a band is playing dance music in the background. Brad stands and offers Katie his hand. "Would you like to dance?"

Katie is in complete happiness as she stands and takes his hand. "I most certainly would kind sir"

The couple dance around the floor enjoying the sensation of being close to each other, Katie wonders about this obviously well-heeled delivery guy until the band finishes. Finishing their drinks they head toward the car park.

Can I give you a lift home or would you prefer a taxi, Katie? Thanks Brad, a lift would be great. On the way out to the car park they are interrupted outside the main entrance by Don and a couple of his cronies.

The smell of alcohol on Don shows he has been drinking heavily as he pushes his way in between them. Grabbing Katie's arm, he begins to drag her away.

"Okay sweetheart, funs over time to go" he says.

Katie, resisting him as best she can exclaim. "Hey, stop, you're hurting me get your hands off me. I'm not going anywhere with you creep."

Brad moves swiftly to undo Dons grip on Katies arm.

"I'm sorry friend but I don't think the lady wants to go any-where with you.

Don gets angry and turns to Brad. "Listen sport she came here with me and she is leaving with me so butt out."

Trying to calm the tension Brad tries to reason with Don.

"Listen, why don't you go and have a drink with your buddies here and leave the lady alone. She doesn't want to go any-where with you, ok?"

Don and his cronies gather around Brad menacingly. Don walks up to Brad and says. "Okay big man this is the way you want to play it. We can play it that way." swinging a punch at Brad which he ducks easily and with a swift Ninjutsu type move he has Don on his back semi-conscious.

"I'm sorry pal, but now will you just go away, please"?

Dons' buddies move in and Brad deals with them one by one as a police cruiser pulls up next to the car park attendant who explains to Alices boyfriend Ben the duty officer, what just happened whilst Brad dusts himself off.

"I'm sorry about all that Katie" as he walks with her towards Ben.

Recognizing Katie. "Well, hello, again Katie, why is it you attract losers like that, pointing to a semi-conscious Don on the ground.

Remonstrating, Katie frowns at Ben. "Ask your girlfriend. That douche bag was her idea." The point taken and knowing that Alice has a matchmaking tendency he turns to Brad.

Point taken Katie. How's it going Brad? Still got it I see, says Ben as he turns to his offsider. Constable, go and cuff that idiot on the ground and let the others know how lucky they were to still be in one piece and take their names."

Katie looked confused. "You two know each other"

Ben smiles broadly. "We certainly do Katie. Brad and I went to school together and joined the Navy together. The difference was he became a Navy Seal. Those clowns picked the wrong guy this time Katie. Are you ok, that idiot didn't hurt you in any way did he."

"I'm fine thanks Ben, but Alice won't be when I get hold of her in the morning." Standing together, they assess the damage and Katie turns to Brad.

"I should say thanks for that but I'm not a big fan of violence." "Neither am I Katie but sometimes we don't have a choice. He will be ok in the morning with just a headache to remind him of his night. I'm more worried about you and don't be too hard on Alice, she means well."

As they chat the car park attendant is pulling up in an exotic vehicle. climbing out he hands Brad the keys. "There you are Sir; we gave it a quick wash whilst it was downstairs."

"Thanks John, how's your mother" Brad says slipping the attendant $50 note.

"Much better thanks. That specialist you sent her to is great. I think she is going to be okay now."

"That's great John, let me know if she needs anything else, okay"?

Brad opens the car door for Katie who is a little confused and befuddled by it all. The car pulls away from the country club and the pair are silent until Katie breaks the silence.

"You're not a delivery man, are you."

"No, I'm not Katie. I own the company. It is a very long story that I need to talk to you about."

"You've got a captive audience Brad, so shoot." She says leaning affectionately across towards Brad.

"For a start, tell me why the hell you're deliveries if you own the company."

"Katie, yours is the only cafe I personally deliver to and that's because I want to see you."

"I'm flattered but why didn't you just come and talk to me or ask me out? I would have gone you know even if you were just the delivery guy. Hey, wait a minute, so that's what you were trying to do that day in the foyer of your building wasn't it? Now I get it."

Brad smiling. "Yes, it was, but my timing was a bit off."

"So, the sponsorship to the competition, your being here tonight, it's all a big game for you isn't it." A hurt look comes over her face as she moves closer to the window of the car. "Brad, you've lied to me you lied to us all along just so you can hit on me. You're no better than that douche bag you flattened outside the club. Let me out of this car right now."

"Katie, you've got it all wrong I need to explain things to you." The car stops at traffic lights. Katie seizes the opportunity to jump out of the car and hail a passing taxi.

Brad yelling out in the open car door. "Wait, wait, Katie, I really do need to talk to you." But it's too late, Katie is in the back of the taxi, crying as it disappears into the distance.

CHAPTER 9

THE RIFT

The next day at the café the ladies aren't speaking as Katie refuses to acknowledge Alice. Deeply hurt by the date Alice set up and all the following incidents she is in a world of emotional pain. She likes Brad but dislikes that he lied to her. Although she now regrets her actions, leaving the car, her initial reaction was influenced by the deception.

Just before the lunchtime rush starts Alice decides to break the icy silence.

"What's eating you today kiddo? How was the date with the bank guy last night?"

With tears in her eyes Katie turns to Alice. "You set me up again and made a fool of me. I don't want anything to do with you ever again." With nowhere to go she runs out into the alley crying. Jeremy walks over to where Alice is standing with Nigel.

"What's with her today, Alice?"

"I don't know guys. Some problem with her date last night as far as I can tell, but surely it can't have been that bad I mean he was a banker. Can you hold the fort while I go and see her?"

"Certainly, take your time, I think she really needs a shoulder right now."

Heading into the alley to comfort her friend, she finds her sitting on her haunches, crying uncontrollably. "Hey Kiddo, don't cry, I'm sorry if it didn't turn out the way you expected and don't forget we've got the competition we booked to go and......."

"I'm not going anywhere with you. In fact, I am leaving the cafe after this shift and I never want to see you or this stinking hole again."

"You can't do that kiddo were a team girlfriend. We belong together" says Alice in a comforting voice.

"Go find yourself another teammate Alice, this girlfriend is off. I've had it." She says storming back into the cafe throwing her apron at Grumbles as she heads to the front door.

Grumbles in typical fashion. "Hey, where do you think you're going Missy!"

"I'm out of here you mean spirit old bastard. You can stick your tired old cafe, disgusting customers, and worn-out machinery up your backside. Grumbles Yells after her. "Hey, you haven't finished your shift yet and I want all those spare aprons back if you're quitting. They cost money, you know."

"Oh! for goodness's sake Grumbles. Can't you see the girls upset" says Nigel as he prepares for the lunch rush. Grumbles retiring to his stockroom mumbles under his breath. Alice chases after Katie who has come to work on her pushbike as usual and is peddling away down the road.

"Katie, stop, let's talk sweetie. Don't let's leave it like this. Come on, Katie." Alice finally gives up the chase, realizing its futile.

Later that Day after her shift is over Ben comes to pick her up and, in the trip, out to his ranch, he can see the Alice is not herself.

"What's the matter Alice, you look like the world has ended."

Might as well Ben, Katie threw in her job and doesn't want anything to do with me or the competition. Seems like her date last night didn't work out and I guess I'm to blame."

"Don't take it to heart sweety, I know what happened with the date: he says and explains the details of the fight and the aftermath. He explained his relationship with Brad and had no idea that Katie was fond of him.

"Well thanks very much Mr. policeman says Alice. When were you going to tell me or us about all this? Can you take me to Katies place please we need to have a chat about all this but for now I need to talk to Katie and see if I can recover our friendship."

The car turns off and heads back to Katies neighborhood. Pulling up outside Alice walks to the front door and knocks. As the curtain pulled aside, Alice is surprised to see Jeremy's face peering out. The front door opens and they hear Katie in the distance yelling that she doesn't want to see anyone.

"Sweety it's me Alice and we need to talk."

"Go Away, we are finished" say Katie obviously still crying.

Walk up the short flight of stairs to Katies bedroom she opens the door. "it's not going to end like this kiddo; you mean too much to me and I'm not sure exactly what happened last night but I'm sure we can fix it. Let us try" she says sitting on the bed and putting a motherly arm around Katies shoulder.

"It's all gone wrong and I can't fix anything my life is a joke and I don't know what to do anymore. Says Katie as she bursts into tears again and nestling into Alices shoulder.

"Cry it out kiddo, cry it out and when your done we will sort it all out" says Alice gently holding the sobbing young woman.

Sometime later Jeremy brings them a tea tray with freshly baked scones. "You goes have been up here for hours and I thought you might be hungry."

Alice and Katie are sitting on the floor with Katies head on Alices shoulder. Alice explained what she knew about the date from what Ben had told her. Katie has explained the unusual relationship with Brad. They agreed that it was not a good start to a relationship and they should go and see Brad to get it all out on the table.

Katie is feeling better and apologises for her outburst at the café and as the two women sit together enjoying Jeremys scones and the cup of tea, he has brought them. They agree Jeremy really is a good baker as they finish off the scones and cuddle more.

That evening Jeremy and Nigel prepare one of their one pot dinner specials and the four of them sit down to enjoy the meal and discuss the issues calmly. Deciding there was no point in confronting Brad but Katie should leave it for him to see Katie.

The contest was still a difficult problem but Nigel pointed out there was fine print in the application form which had consequences for applicants that pulled out within 14 days of the competition. As it was less than 5 days away, they felt obliged to continue.

CHAPTER 10

THE CONTEST

The two ladies reconciled their differences realizing they had signed a contract and obliged to go to the Baristas contest regardless of their personal feeling. The flight was still an uneasy thing as the forced attendance did not sit well with Katie who had built up considerable resentment toward Brad finding out he was a major sponsor and was behind the enforcement of the contest contract and rules. Alice is ambivalent and happy to be with her old friend despite the icy circumstances.

Meanwhile, back in Summerton the day after the competition started, Brad pulls into Bens's ranch having confirmed with his marketing manager that the girls were in fact at the Barista competition and not likely to be at the ranch.

The day is sunny and bright. Ben has a day off and is enjoying introducing Alice's daughter Kim to the horses. Looking out from the stable doors he sees a familiar car entering his driveway.

Walking out to greet Brad he leaves Kim with his part time stable hand John who also works at the country club parking cars. Kim and John are about the same age and seem to be getting on well.

"John, can you show Kim the tack room and where we keep all the riding gear, please. I've got to see our visitor." John nods and Kim smiles at John.

Wiping his hands Ben strolls over to the exotic car as Brad gets out.

"Hi Brad, what brings you out to the countryside today."

Ben I've got a problem, I need to talk to you about, its most important."

"Sure Brad, I heard that you enforced the contract they signed with your company. Man, Katie is one unhappy lady not to mention the ear bashing I got from Alice. Being forced to participate, I'm unsure if they'll perform well at the contest. For what it's worth old friend, I think you have ruined any chance of a relationship with Katie and mine with Alice is not that happy either."

Walking into the ranch house with Ben, Brad realizes what a loyal friend he has in Ben.

"Ben, I know it's all a bit confusing and distressing but I figured there was no other way to get those two together. They're made for each other and they know what they're doing with Coffee. I'm sorry if it's caused you and Alice any pain, she's a good lady. Ben, I really need your help with something though, its most important."

Ben walks the pair into a very open ranch style living room and heads toward the kitchen.

"Don't worry about us Brad, Alice and I are getting on fine. In fact, I might have something to ask you about once all this contest stuff is done and dusty. You any good at weddings old friend"

Opening the refrigerator, he turns to Brad. "That's for another day, let's see if we can solve your problems. Let's have a beer and you can tell me all about it. The look of astonishment on Brads face says it all. You're a sly old dog, Ben. I thought you were a confirmed bachelor.

"Well, you know how it goes Brad. The right one comes along you don't let them go. Might be a good lesson in that saying for you Brad." He hands Brad an Icy cold beer and they clink the bottles together. "Maybe Ben, maybe"

Back at the Baristas contest the ladies are powering through the minor heats and have reached the semi-finals. Katie is still not talking to Alice, but their training and years of teamwork are paying off in-spite of the icy off-stage relationship.

The announcement that four teams had made it through to the semifinals including the Coffee Maidz team of Alice and Katie met with jubilation.

Later that day, after reality had set in, Katie took Alice aside and they went to the bar for a drink. Alice could feel a definite softening in Katies tone and was curious to sit with her and find out what had changed.

Katie extended her hand, silently sharing the moment.

"Alice, I'm sorry for the way I have been carrying on. You didn't deserve it and I hope we can move on from it."

"Katie, girlfriend, your like a sister to me and I'm so happy we can put all this behind us but I've got know what was upsetting you so much"?

"My life hasn't turned out the way I hoped it would and it seemed like everyone was lying to me and laughing at me. I don't have much to give except my friendship and affection and it just seemed like everyone was taking advantage of that. When I found out that Brad had lied about his role in the coffee contest and his overall wealth it was just the final straw for me.

The whole blind date fiascos, Grumbles, the nerds all took a toll on me and I wanted to lash out and you, my dear friend, received most of it I'm afraid. The other night I was sitting in our room when you were downstairs. I was looking out the window and saw a couple walking down the street holding hands and enjoying each other's company. I dawned on me that my problem was relationships or the lack of them.

I know you saw that sadness in me and tried to help. The fact that it didn't work out was nothing to do with you but with my fear of disappointment and I realised that you were the one person in my life that was trying to help me."

Alice, you are very dear to me and I don't want to lose you over something silly.

The two women embrace and hold each other close for a long time. Alice breaks the silence. "Okay, so what say we get on and win this competition."

"Absolutely girlfriend, but for now I need another drink." Signaling to the barman to bring 2 more they settle into discussions about how to win this thing. Later, sitting on her own Alice calls Ben.

"Hi sweetheart, how are you and Kim getting on."

"She is having a ball and John has given her a basic riding lesson."

"That's great she loves horses. "Who is John" asks Alice?

"He is the lad from the country club carpark. He's a nice young guy so how's the contest going" asks Ben.

Pausing for few moments "Well yes, the contest is going fine, we are in the semis, but the atmosphere between Katie and myself has changed from being as cold as a polar bears arse. We had a long chat and its all good" hearing talking in the background she recognised Brads voice.

"Sorry Sweetheart I didn't know you had company, say hello to Brad, the bastard who put us in this contract mess. Just kidding, don't say that I understand why he enforced the contract on us. Love you, see you in a couple of days or sooner if we drop out."

The day started bright and early with Katie and Alice taking advantage of an early start to walk and chatting about their strategy out of the earshot of other competitors.

The semifinals go off without a hitch and the ladies put on a stellar performance wowing the judges and attracting a lot of media attention.

Their finals announcement received hugs and high-fives. There is a long lunch break before the finals, so Alice decides to have one more try at her ideas for a winning brew.

"Katie, can you believe we have made it into the Finals. One more hurdle and we could be Baristas of the year. You know what that means, TV appearances, our own brand of coffee, machines with our signatures on them and a decent chunk of cash to boot. After lunch lets together and discuss our plans for the finals and my brew ideas."

Katie looks at Alice, I know what you want to discuss and you've been right all the way through the contest so let's go with it. It will mean we will have to work as one and the clock will be ticking so let's use the Columbian mix, Ill fine grind, you brew and steam whilst I get the additive sorted.

The pair cuddle and arm in arm head in for lunch. "We have a real chance to win this contest girlfriend" says Alice. lunching together they work out the strategy on a napkin. According to observers in the know and onlookers, they stand strong chances of winning.

Walking back to the competition area Alice turns to Katie. "I'm sorry I messed you around with all those losers Katie, I should have realized my taste in men has never been all that great."

touching Katies arm tenderly as they stroll back to the contest.

With a smile on her face Katie turns to Alice. "That's an understatement, first it was the dog fur nerd then the Gestapo banker. Geez Louise, what were you thinking." They both laugh and see the funny side of the tragic blind dates.

"Whilst we are talking about our love lives Alice, what's happening with your cop, he's a nice guy."

Alice looking down and acting shy. "I think he's going to pop the question Katie and I think my answer will be yes. But hey you knew that's where it was heading didn't you?"

Smiling and putting an arm around her friend Katie responds "Yes, I had my suspicions right after he showed you, his truncheon." Alice taps Katies arm, "your awful Katie, but what about you and Brad? He would be a great catch and he obviously likes you."

Pausing for a moment Katie responds. "I'm not sure Alice, he lied to me, forced me to go on this contest, made out he was a delivery man." Interjecting Alice says. "Kiddo, you know he forced us to go to this contest to bring us back together. He's also a shy guy and I think he masqueraded as a delivery guy so he wouldn't scare you off. Give him a chance. I know my advice has been a bit off with regards to men, but I think he deserves another chance."

Katie nods, "well maybe, but I'm fed up with men and their games."

The pair are busy working out their blend and style for the finals when a young, well-dressed man with boyish good looks approaches the ladies. Standing beside the pair he says.

"Hi, I've been watching your performances in the contest and I'm impressed.

Katie looks at Alice with fire in her eyes.

"Is this another one of your stunts, do I have to put up with another one of your tosser mates that keep making a bloody nuisance of themselves and messing up my life?"

Alice shrugs then stand to confront the young man.

"Listen sport I don't know what you're game is but whatever it is we are not buying right."

The young man passes over a card to Katie.

"Ladies I assure you both this is not a game and I'm not here to hit on you I have a business proposition to put to you."

Alice, standing close to the young man in an intimidating fashion. "You think we need some money or something and you want a threesome is that what you've got a mind you dirty bastard."

Meanwhile Katie picks up the card and reads it.

"Wait, Wait. I think he's legit Alice."

Looking at the young man and back to Alice.

"This is Dan Edwards CEO Coffee International Enterprises, I've seen his picture in Barista Monthly."

Alice trying to defend Katies honor and assure her the unexpected visit from the young man was not her doing.

"Oh, I suppose he was the centerfold was he."

"No Alice, sit down and stop making a scene. This is one of the top coffee guys in the country and he runs a multi-million, dollar distribution business. Please, Mr. Edwards, ignore my friend.

"It's been a tough competition and I think the strain has got to her. Turning to her friend, go grab us another coffee and we can hear what Mr. Edwards has to say."

"Please, call me Dan. Mr. Edwards sounds like my father who started the business as a buyer."

Alice has left to get more coffee for the table as Katie sits considering the young man sitting opposite her.

"Your father was a coffee buyer"? Asks Katie.

"Yes, he was one of the first to start blending Columbian and arabica beans with the rare New Guinea coffee beans."

"Wait a minute was your father's name Tom?

Katie nodding as Dan replies,

"I think my father worked with your father as a buyer. He always spoke about the brilliant Tom Edwards. That's amazing Katie, may I call you Katie asks Dan.

Alice returns to the table with the coffees.

"Here we are guys; I think the girls behind the counter were a little intimidated by my request when the recognized me. You two look like you're getting on well, what have I missed."

"Nothing Alice we seem to have common grounds in coffee, no pun intended."

They laugh and settle down to business with papers and figures spread out and deep in discussion. An obvious sexual tension is developing between Katie and the young man as their eyes meet.

After the meeting and Dans departure Alice turns to Katie.

"Well kiddo that went well, what do you think. I mean apart from the long stares you were giving each other."

"Stop it Alice it was just business, right."

"Ok, just business, winking at Katie.

The tension broken; Katie wants to change their focus as she grabs Alice's arm. "Come on Alice lets go win this damn competition and get home."

At the Baristas competition the contestants wait anxiously for the bell to start. Alice and Katie are ready to perform and are all geared up for what they need to do.

An envelope is given to Alice, who acknowledges it with a wink at Katie, assuming these are the instructions for the final round. The officer waits beside them as Alice smiling opens the envelope. Her expression changes from smiles to disbelief causing Katie to ask what's up.

With a blank look on her face, Alice hands Katie the envelope.

"Katie we are disqualified."

"No! surely not. What for she shouts as she turns to the official for an answer.

The official speaks using a microphone announcing the disqualification to the assembled media and audience.

"Sorry ladies, but it's been found that you used alcohol in one of your coffees during the semi-finals." Under section 17 of the rules, it clearly says." He never got to finish his announcement.

Alice jumps up and grabs the microphone.

"Fuck you and fuck your competition."

She throws a bin of used coffee grounds at the official and sweeps the prep table clear of cups and saucers which crash to the ground. The official, covered in used coffee grounds and milk waste tries to calm the situation as cameras flash and a local TV station records the debacle.

"Ladies, ladies please compose yourself. This is a public place and formal competition of high standing."

Katie now joins the fray.

"Compose this arsehole."

Tipping milk over the official as camera's flash and security guards rushes up to wrestle the ladies to the ground. Other contestants run for cover as the two start throwing cups and anything else, they can get their hands on at the hapless officials and security guards.

Down in the audience the competitors are cheering them on and laughing at each hit. Eventually, the ladies were removed from the venue and accompanied back to their hotel room. Sitting at the window with a mix of coffee and milk in her hair, Alice turns to Katie.

"Well, that was fun kiddo."

The pair look at one another for a minute and burst into laughter.

"I guess we blew it" says Katie still laughing.

CHAPTER 11

THE HOME COMING

T he next day the pair are sitting silently in the airport departure lounge. Occasionally people whisper and point towards the two ladies. Alice sticks her tongue out at an elderly couple whispering to each other and looking her way. Katie opens a local paper to hide behind until she sees the front page.

"Oh goody, look we made the papers. You promised me fame; l we got it grandma." Handing the newspaper to Alice. The picture of them on the front page struggling with security guards in very compromising positions. The headlines read Baristas go ballistic.

"Well kiddo, that's your 15 min of fame, but I guess that's the end of the coffee shop deal with Dan Edwards" says Katie looking more despondent.

"I guess so Katie, they won't want our kind of publicity associated with their brand."

The pair sit in silence till boarding time. As they enter the plane the flight attendant speaks quietly.

"Welcome aboard ladies, loved what you did to those pompous arseholes."

Taking their seats at the back of the plane Alice turns to Katie with a smile.

"Anyway, we've always got old grumbles to go back to."

"I think we burnt that bridge, but anyway we will see what else we can do when we get back home. I'm optimistic but I can't work out why."

The flight home was uneventful except for the flight attendants and others asking the ladies for their autographs and apologizing for the in-flight coffee. After landing the ladies walk through the terminal having picked up their bags from the carousel.

A police officer stops them and instructs them to please come with him.

Alice speaks out first.

"What's this all about officer, are we under arrest, is this to do with the Baristas competition."

Cameras flash as the local media takes photographs of the two women being escorted from the airport by law enforcement officers.

"Terrific grandma, now we are hometown celebrities for all the wrong reasons."

"Don't worry kiddo, I'm sure it's a mistake. They could have arrested us after the competition if they wanted and besides this is another states authority."

Katie frowning, "why don't I feel relieved to know that."

In a stern voice, the Police Officer instructs them to follow him as he leads them towards a parked patrol car and opens a backdoor.

Alice begins protesting again.

"Listen officer unless you tell me what this is all about, we aren't getting in the car."

The police officer responds.

"Please don't make a scene lady, it is just a routine enquiry."

The passenger side front door opens, and Ben appears smiling.

Alice is delighted.

"You big softy, I thought we were in trouble. What's the squad car pickup all about are we in trouble."

Ben smiles and points to the open back door of the patrol car.

"You will be if you don't get in the car. I'll explain later. You first Katie you've got a be in the middle."

Puzzled, Katie slides into the middle rear seat to find Brad next to her tries to get out but Alice is blocking her exit as the door slams shut behind them.

Katie is frantically pulling on the door handles.

"Let me out of this car now or I'm going to scream the place down."

The patrol car speeds away with lights on making a clear passage for them to exit the busy airport. From the front seat Ben lowers a security screen and announces that the back doors don't open from the inside ladies

"I suggest you relax sit back and listen to the man beside you. He has a lot to tell you two, and Alice, we need to talk when I get you home."

Brad tries to ease the situation with a tearful Katie sitting beside him.

"Katie, I know you're upset, and I heard about the contest."

Waving a local newspaper, he points to a picture on the cover, Alice grabs the paper and exclaims.

"My oh my, look how our fame has spread, even to our own hometown."

Katie frowns at Alice and stares angrily at Brad.

"I think I've heard all I need to from you Brad. I trust this is not another one of Alice's ploys. If it is, then you and I are done for good, Alice. I'm sick of your match making misadventures."

Brad senses that he is losing her attention and decides he must be decisive, or he will lose her for good.

"Katie, listen to me, it's not a ploy or anything else, trust me it's very important that we talk. I figured this was the only way I could. So, I asked Ben for his help."

Katie realizes she can't go anywhere so might as well get it over and done with so she can go back to her miserable existence.

"Okay Brad, I guess I'm not about to go anywhere so get on with it, so I can get on with what's left of my dysfunctional life."

Brad stares hard at Katie as he prepares to drop his bombshell.

"Katie, you need to know that I am your brother."

Katies look of disbelief crosses her face.

"What, have you been taking something naughty and that's why you're in this police cruiser. No, you're just winding me up in some sick practical joke set up by Her" she says pointing to Alice.

Brad forcefully cuts her off in a fashion she had not seen him do before.

"Katie, just sit and listen please. Our parents died in a car accident when I was five and you were three. We were both adopted by different people and moved to different parts of the country. It's just coincidence that we both wound up here near each other."

Cynically, Katie waves her hands around in magician type gestures.

"That sounds like a fairytale to me, nice try though."

Brad hands her a birth certificate.

"I thought you might think something like that, but this is your birth certificate Katie, and this is mine. Do you still think it's a fairytale?

The patrol car speeds off into the afternoon sun, Katie study's the paperwork and hands it to Alice.

This information appears credible. I have always been aware of my adoption, but I held deep affection for my adoptive parents and never felt the need to investigate my origins further. So why do you have to bring this up now?

Looking serious and with a tinge of sorrow in his voice he looks directly into Katie eyes.

"I'm dying Katie. I have terminal cancer and they give me less than a year to live."

Katie sits in stunned silence. An air of gloom has fallen over the inside of the patrol car.

Looking for the right words to say Katie stumble the words out.

"That's terrible, awful. What can I do for you Brad? I feel terrible, I'm sorry I have been so elusive and rude to you. I feel dreadful. How can I make it up to you?"

With a gentle hand on hers and soft voice he says

"Spend some time with me and get to know me. Also, I want you to take over the company Katie.

A look of astonishment on her face Katie turns to Brad.

"What!! I can't do that! I mean, I'm just a coffee lady and a failed one of that."

Holding up the newspaper to demonstrate her failure.

Alice nudges Katie. "You can do this kiddo, I'm sure you would be great at it.

Cutting across their thoughts Brad says

"Katie and Alice, I've got to tell you why you lost the competition. Everyone knew the fix was in. The opposition got wind of my illness and wanted to take over the Company at a bargain basement price. They couldn't have a pair of award-winning Baristas attached to the sale price. Unfortunately, you both overreacted and the rest is history. But there is a saying. There is no such thing as bad publicity, so don't worry too much about the fallout "

Alice is studying the newspaper.

"Thank goodness I had clean knickers on that day."

Smiling at Alice, Katie responds.

"That's a relief I suppose. That's your best angle."

They High five as Alice says.

"Touché girlfriend"

The mood has lightened as Ben turns around to talk with the trio in the back seat.

"Folks, we are heading to the ranch for dinner and a long chat, Okay."

Later that night after a wonderful spit roast cooked by Alices daughter Kim and boyfriend John, they relax in the outdoor setting looking over the ranch toward the mountains in the distance.

Alice, Ben, and the two youngsters engage in conversation while Brad speaks with Katie privately as they walk toward the barn.

"Katie, I know you need to think about what I said in the patrol car today but you need to know that I have no family my parents are dead, and I've never married so you're all I have.

If you don't take over the company, I will have no choice but to sell out which means the buyers will certainly move the operations elsewhere and everyone will be out of a job."

Overwhelmed by it all Katie responds quietly.

"Brad, I don't know anything about your business or what you do. I wouldn't know where to start and I'm not sure your team would welcome me as their boss."

"That's no problem, Katie, you know coffee, that's for sure, and I have a good management team to help you with the other parts of the business. If you agree I will need you to come in as soon as possible before I start my chemotherapy in a week or so.

"You can learn the ropes and I'll have people show you how the business runs and who you should go to for advice and help in the industry."

"I'm a bit overwhelmed by all this Brad, but I guess if you think I can pull it off I should at least give it a go." With tears in her eyes.

"I'm concerned about you though. Is there any chance you might pull through."

"No chance I'm afraid, its eating me away and there is only palliative care for my future now. Our time is running out and there is so much I need to tell you and show you. Can you move into my house with me so we can spend time together?"

Katie nods agreement and wipes away a tear as she hugs Brad.

"It's going to be alright Katie. I've already had a long chat with my senior management team and they are looking forward to helping you and keeping the business here in the town. In fact, we are all going to have dinner at my place at the weekend so you can meet them all in casual surrounding.

They are good folks and they've been with the business for years. They won't let you down.

"Also, as I'm leaving the house to you, you will be able to check out the facilities whilst your there and make any changes you want."

"Brad, I don't want to think about that right now as she hugs her brother Brad.

Going back to the house and joining the group on the deck, Alice is first to speak.

"Well, have decisions been made, all good I hope Katie" says Alice.

Wiping her eyes, she puts her hands on Brads shoulder.

"I guess so folks. Looks like I'm going to be the next CEO of Brads company."

Brad interrupts her. "No Katie. It's going to be your company, right."

"That's great news for you both even though the circumstances could be better. However, we have an announcement to."

Katie, knowing what its likely she rushes to Alice and flings her arms around her.

"Congratulations you two.

"But we haven't told you the news, yet Katie" says Ben?

"You don't have to, I can see the twinkle in Alice's eyes, she all aglow and that can only mean one thing apart from a special coffee she makes."

"Thanks Katie, no more special coffee tips for you Kiddo" says Alice.

With his hands up alike a traffic cop Ben formally makes the announcement.

"Ok I guess the surprise is over. We are getting married in a couple of months or so. Katie, we would love you be my maiden of honor?"

"Of- course I will grandma" says Katie as they hug each other again.

"Enough of the grandma stuff already "says Alice.

'Okay, no more Kiddo and no more grandma right" says Katie holding out her hand.

"I guess I don't need to ask who the best man will be Ben. Says Katie,

"Come here and give me a hug. I'm so happy for both of you. Hey, we can have the reception at Grumbles Café."

Laughing and chasing Katie around the room Alice says.

"Not fucking likely kiddo, you're not planning my wedding reception if that's your idea of how it should be done. The pair laugh and cuddle as Katie reminds her of the pact not to use kiddo and grandma anymore.

CHAPTER 12

NEW BEGINNINGS

In the coming weeks Katie is busy learning the business and meeting with the managers. She is surprised at how well she has taken to her new role and gets on well with the management team. Brad appears occasionally in a wheelchair when he can, but his condition is getting worse.

One morning at Alice and Bens ranch, the phone rings. Picking up the phone she says

"Who, sorry, who is it? Oh Dan, how are you? Long time no speak! I thought you had abandoned us after our catastrophic performance at the Baristas Competition."

Listening carefully, she responds.

"Okay Dan, yes, I will call her, sure. Yes, I still have your card. OK, I will let you know. Bye."

With a puzzled look on her face, she hangs up and turns to Ben making them lunch on his day off.

"Darling I've got a go out."

She picks up her car keys and heads out the door.

Taken by surprise, Ben looks up.

"What about our lunch? What's so urgent."

"I won't be long Ben. I'll explain later."

20 minutes later Alice pulls up outside of Katies offices and strides in waving to the receptionist as she heads towards Katie's office. Katie is on the phone but hangs up and moves around to embrace Alice.

"Alice this is a pleasant surprise, what brings you to town."

"Katie you'll never guess who just called me."

Hand on her chin and a pensive look on her face

"Let me guess, Grumbles wants you back and he has sent you to recruit me as well. So, when do we start, I can't wait."

Alice realising Katie is being silly, waves her hands at her.

"Do you remember that nice young guy we met at the Baristas contest that wanted to collaborate with us on expanding his coffee shop chain? "

A quizzical look crosses Katie's face as she recalls the meeting.

"I remember him he was a bit of a hunk as well as being quite a good businessperson as I recall. Let me think, yes, Daniel was his name as I recall, Daniel Edwards."

She picks up a trade magazine from the end of her desk.

"Yes, here he is and there's a picture and article about his growing empire."

Motioning toward the lounge beside her desk Alice says

"Okay girlfriend, sit and take a breath. Daniel is in town and he wants to see us both. The deal is still on the table and he hasn't forgotten you either kiddo." winking at Katie.

"Hey, I thought we agreed to drop the kiddo thing Grandma" says Katie with a sarcastic smile on her Face.

Nonetheless, circumstances have significantly evolved since the initial proposal was presented. I mean I'm flat out here with this."

Holding up her hand to Katies lips Alice cuts across Katies talk.

"Here you go again always negative. I thought you would be more positive now. Here you are sitting in a big office, with a great business and lovely home and you're still cynical.

"Listen Katie the guy is genuine, you've met him, his original deal was great and he's a hunk! What more do you want?"

With a thoughtful look on her face Katie responds

"Okay, Alice. I guess you're right, it won't hurt to listen."

Rubbing her hands together before cuddling Katie Alice says

"That's my girl, I'll arrange for us to meet him for dinner tonight at the club with Ben and I at seven thirty."

Stunned by the reappearance of Daniel and the deal re surfacing after the competition, Katie sits in her office considering her options.

A phone call interrupts her thoughts as she takes a call from Brads nurse.

It was bad news about Brads condition which has worsened and left him bedridden, sedated, and unresponsive. Pausing for a moment after hanging up she called out to her assistant.

"Josie, can you arrange a management team meeting for this afternoon please."

That night on the way to the club Katie explains to Ben and Alice the situation with Brad deteriorating health, explaining this was the agreed time Brad would completely sign the business over to Katie and as he would be unable to complete the transition if he waited any longer. Also, there were legal hurdles that would occur if they waited any longer.

The car park attendant recognised Katie as she got out of the car and smiled.

"Good evening Maam"

Pausing to chat with the young man

"How's it going Eric, how's college" says Katie.

Smiling broadly Eric responds

"I should graduate in another year and I hope to do some post grad work after that. The scholarship funds sure made life easier."

"Glad we were able to help and don't forget we are always looking for bright young people. You know you will always have a job with me if you want it." says Katie as she joins Alice and Ben.

Smiling Eric takes the keys from Ben.

"Thanks' Maam I really do appreciate that offer and all you've done for us and the town."

With a lady on each arm, they stroll off toward the club's entrance.

Eric runs up behind them,

"I almost forgot. A man was looking for you Miss Katie. He said he booked a private dining room and you were to ask at the desk inside."

Puzzled Katie thanks Eric as they head off into the club.

Whilst Ben is busy arranging for a table Alice whispers to Katie.

"Hope you've got your red knickers on so he will recognize you from the Newspapers front page."

Katie taps her affectionately on the arm.

"You really haven't changed have you. Anyway, you're taken grandma. This one's mine regardless of the business deal. OK?"

"That a girl, just let me know when you're going to do some lap dancing for him, so I can take my desert and leave you to it."

Quick to respond Katie says.

"I remember table dancing was your specialty, Alice. Didn't think much of your choice of venue though." As she smiles benignly at Alice.

Feigning shock Alice responds.

"Don't tell me you found out about that little episode with Grumbles and Mona and the tape?"

Nodding Katie steps closer to Alice

"Yep, I certainly did Alice, you remember Jeremy and Nigel? Well, they found the backup tape after someone tipped them off and now, they both work for me. Power has its advantages you know."

Alice looks a bit sheepish and embarrassed but Katie quickly puts her fears to rest.

"It's ok Alice, it was all in a good cause and your misdemeanor is safe with me. However, I think Grumbles still wonders about the location of that tape."

Ben returns announcing the table is all sorted but before they head off to the dining room Alice turns Katie around in the opposite direction facing a corridor.

"The private dining room is down there. Don't keep your future business partner waiting sweetie."

Looking a little confused Katie stands looking back as Ben and Alice to walk off into the restaurant waving as they go.

"Where are you sending me."

Alice pauses still holding Bens's hand, she turns to Katie with wry smile on her face.

"I'm sending you into your future girlfriend. You're on your own from here on Kiddo. Ben and I are having dinner in the dining room, your future is in there."

She says pointing toward a sign which says private dining rooms this way.

Confused, Katie turns and starts walking toward Alice and Ben

"But what about the business deal we are supposed to negotiate. Hang on, don't tell me this is another one of your setups Alice?"

"Don't worry about all the business stuff kiddo, Dan and I put that together earlier today and the plan is to meet with you and your management committee tomorrow to thrash out the details."

With her hands on Katies shoulders Alice looks deep into Katies eyes.

"I'm your development manager for your business and the merger is logical. The merged business means you're going to be the exclusive supplier to the Coffee Stopz chain globally and that deal alone is worth millions to your company and will secure its future. But it's all subject to your approval so don't blow it tonight, figuratively speaking I mean," says Alice, smiling naughtily.

"You cunning bitch. How did you know I would go for that sort of deal and why the dinner ploy?" says Katie with a hurt look on her face.

"Listen to grandma this time. Sweetheart, this type of deal is all you've been talking about since you took over the business and besides, it means we will be working closely, so it will be like old times but without old grumble bum riding your arse.

"The dinner was Daniels idea not mine. I think he fancies you! Now stop messing about and go get him tiger." Says

Alice patting Katie on the backside and pushing her toward the private dining area before striding off to join Ben in the restaurant.

Walking down the corridor Katie takes a deep breath before entering the private dining room with a sign saying, 'Daniel Edwards Party' marked on the door."

Entering the room, she locked eyes with Daniel as he rose to greet her. The dinner was more than food and the attraction between the two was obvious as they chatted long into the evening. As the club was closing Daniel drove Katie home and stops at her front door, turning to Katie next to him in the car with a look of affection and anticipation in his eyes.

"I hope we can do this again, Katie," he says.

The events of the evening had changed Katie and she found herself deeply attracted to this handsome man. e seizing the moment she kisses him. The long passionate kiss sealed their fate as more than just business partners.

The couple spent the next few days balancing work and their relationship. It was observed that the bond between the two individuals strengthened, and their relationship was viewed positively by others.

The couple frequently visited Brad, discussing the deal and its progress beside his bed. Asking Katie to stay one day Brad held out his hand to her.

"You look happy Katie, is he the one?"

"I think so, we work well together and enjoy each other's company. I think you can say we love each other and lets see where that all leads" says Katie holding Brads hand.

"I'm very happy for you sis, just make sure your relationship with Dan doesn't cloud your mind for business. I hope your mind is clear about this merger as it's a great deal you've worked out. I just want you to be sure that your relationship is not bound in some way to the deal."

Katie is a little taken aback but understands what Brad means.

"Brad, the deal is for the company. If I sensed anything false connected to the business deal with Dan, I would pull us out tomorrow. I've tested that theory already and have some outs built into the contracts.

"On the relationship side, I keep that separate even though it's obvious we care for each other so rest easy brother" she says kissing Brad on the forehead and leaves to join Dan in the lounge room.

The Wedding

A month later Ben and Alice's wedding was a wonderful event and set the scene for their future together. The town turned out to see the bride and groom travel through town on a horse drawn carriage led by a police escort after getting married in the local church.

Katie and Kim as the bridesmaids along with the groomsmen Daniel and John followed in a convertible with an oversized fake coffee pot on the bonnet. The wedding party was transported from the outskirts of town to a bus and proceeded to the ranch for the reception.

The large barn down near the lake had been set up under the direction of Jeremy and Nigel and it had the look of a country music festival. A band was set up on a stage in one corner and the catering in another. Except for an area set up as a dance floor there were tables set up for the wedding guests with a long table at the rear of the barn for the wedding party.

The bus bringing the wedding party took a long scenic route so that guests who attended the wedding ceremony in town had time to get to the ranch before they arrived.

Police in full uniform lined the entrance to the barn and raised their outstretched arms to form an arch with fake coffee pots in their hands, tipping these as the bride and groom passed under them spilling confetti on the happy couple.

Jeremy acted as MC and did a wonderful job whilst Nigel made sure the food service and drinks were on time. A large screen positioned behind the wedding party table facilitated speeches and well-wishes, allowing messages to be conveyed effectively.

Brad was too sick to attend but gave a wonderful speech from his bed via a link.

"Grandma, you've been a big part of my life in recent times and I'm so pleased you've taken care of kiddo sitting there staring daggers at me. For those who have been on another planet you should know that these two ladies are the finest Baristas on the planet. I'm sorry Alice that I couldn't be there but I have sent a parcel of special cookies for you to enjoy" the crowd understating the joke giggles as he continues.

"Ben, I know you've made Alice very happy and I'm sure the story about police truncheons will be told by someone else, Daniel, when are you going to make an honest woman out of my sister, No pressure right. Enjoy your night and your life together, I'm thinking of you all and wish I could have had a dance with you Alice and Katie. Love you all."

With hands trembling, Brad blows a kiss and the screen goes blank. The crowd remains quiet for a moment, realising this is the last time they will see Brad.

Meal over and the many speeches made it was time for some fun and dancing. The bridal party had changed into more comfortable attire in preparation for square dancing. The event featured a mix of line dancing, including the Nutbush dance, and more intimate, slow dances. Katie enjoyed that part of the night as Daniel held her close as she nestled onto his shoulder.

As the evening came to an end and the happy couple waved away in a limo to a high mountain resort for their wedding night Daniel and Katie sat amongst the hay bales at the edge of the barn. Daniels' arm around Katie showed his devotion and care.

Katie was the first to speak, looking up at Daniel.

"That was a great wedding wasn't it."

"Sure, was Kiddo" he says smiling as she playfully taps him on the arm, and he playfully wrestles her amongst the hay bales leading to a long and passionate kiss.

Sitting Katie holds Daniels face in her hands.

"As much as I would love a roll in the hay with you. Can I remind you we have the ranch house to ourselves tonight" ending her offer with another long kiss.

The deal made Daniel grab an unopened bottle of champagne as he leads Katie out of the barn and up to the ranch house with his arm around her shoulder.

CHAPTER 13

CHANGES

After the wedding and with life as a married couple, Alice and Ben settled into a happy life. Alice's daughter Kim moved in during her college breaks. They enjoy riding with her onto the surrounding hills and camping out became the family's favourite past time.

Ben was promoted before the wedding and now manages the local police command. Alice is pleased as it means less stress and exposure to danger for him as well as more time at home with her.

Her role at work has expanded and she travels frequently to look at the development of the ever-expanding Coffee Stopz cafes and restaurants as well as the commercial kitchen supply centres. Business is good and has expanded past any of their wildest dreams. It has been a hectic time for Alice and Katie who still have great personal and business relationships.

A Sad Day

Brads time finally ran out and he died with Katie and Alice beside him one gloomy morning. Despite expecting it, Katie and Alice were deeply affected by its finality. It was some time before they were able to make the funeral arrangements and the business became a second obligation with the capable managers understanding and taking up the slack.

Brad's funeral was a town affair with all the town flags lowered to half-mast and many businesses shut in remembrance of the man who had help the town so much. The church was filled, with many standing outsides to listen to the service and pay their respects as the coffin arrived.

The burial was a private event attended by Alice, Ben, Katie, Daniel, and a small group of mourners. They stood around the burial site in the rain, holding each other as the coffin was lowered into the ground. A Clergyman is speaking in soft tones under an umbrella.

"We commit our brother Brad's body to the ground may he rest in peace."

The ceremony over the small gathering walked back to the waiting cars with tears flowing as Alice and Katie embraced.

It's clear that Brad had left an indelible mark on the town and to those closest to him. The unspoken thought between Alice and Katie is that nothing will be the same again without Brad around and it takes some days for Katie to accept the fact that he has gone.

Dan is beside her all the time and comforts her as she comes to accept the facts and move on as Brad would have wanted her to do.

A year later at the ranch, Kim, now a beautiful young woman is riding confidently around a paddock with John on another horse. Katie is swapping notes with Alice about the business as they watch the young couple ride around the paddock. Ben and Dan are busy in the background at the barbeque, incinerating some meat as Alice puts it.

Turning to her friend Katie says,

"They make a nice couple don't they Alice."

Smiling back and putting her arm around Katie

"Don't tell me you're going to take over my match making role Kiddo" she says laughing.

"No chance of that grandma, you're the expert, but what do you think of the possibilities there." As she points toward the happy couple riding around the paddock.

"I don't know; they are both young and thinking of their careers and stuff. It will work out. I'm not pushing it."

"That'll make a change for you. I thought you might have wanted to have the formal title of Grandma" Katie says tapping Alice's shoulder.

"That's enough of that kiddo. Anyway, when are you and Dan going to do something about formalizing your relationship" says Alice poking Katie in the ribs playfully?

"Alice, you know I'm over the moon with Daniel, he's a wonderful man and it's been great since we merged the two companies and he took over the chair. I love him dearly and the business is booming. You should know that Mrs. Consultant." Katie says with a business look on her face.

"We've certainly come a long way since our days at Grumbles old dump of a cafe." Says Alice

Turning excitedly to Alice, Katie says

"I meant to tell you; we bought the old cafe and the bakery and the alley behind it. We're funding Jeremy and Nigel to develop the bakery side and we've already taken down the adjoining wall. Dan thinks we should turn the alley into a covered outdoor internet spot, and I suggested we call it Nerd alley which he liked when I told him it's got history."

Swishing the drink in her had Alice asks

"Do you know what happened to old Grumbles and the homeless guy Katie.

"Well Alice, when the dust settled after the Feds investigation into the local mayor and his cohort's fraud and embezzlement case a lot of the bad apples went to jail or took off for other pastures having done deals with the Feds.

"Grumbles decided to retire to Florida when his pedophilia case got waved away in return for evidence against his cousins. The homeless guy isn't homeless anymore. He works for us. Turns out he was a big-time investment banking type when he refused to go along with the corrupt regime under the mayor. Their retribution hit him hard and he lost everything."

"He is a very shrewd financial advisor. Next time your passing drop by and say hello to him, He has the name on his door spelled out in special Cookies, you can't miss it."

The pair burst into laughter.

"That I've got to see girlfriend," says Alice.

"Whilst we are reminiscing Katie, I wonder what happened to those nerds and the banker wanker I set you up with. I'm still sorry about that you know."

"Don't give it a second-thought girlfriend. I don't miss the possibilities of dog hair clothing or nightly beatings." Says Katie

Coming over to announce dinner is ready Dan says.

"What's all this about dog hair and beatings ladies" asks Daniel.

I will explain it to you someday darling but for now let's eat, we are both hungry. Says Katie

"Already ladies, Ben is just fixing the salad and the steaks are ready." Waving his hands to signal the two youngsters in the paddock to come in for lunch, they head into the dining room.

Ben leans close to the two ladies as they are sitting at the table.

"Just so you know ladies," said Ben in a quiet voice. "

"The nerds all left town after their little affray in the alley. Even the Mayor disowned his son after he was caught in a federal case, so he's gone too. Don, who previously faced legal trouble for theft, now works as a toilet attendant and cleaner at the country club.

"I bet that sorted out his attitude as well as his nether regions. I guess that's justice, Coffee Maidz style eh Katie" says Alice.

"By the way girlfriend, after lunch It's your turn to make the coffee Katie, but no special cookies please and just a regular brew without the additives" says Alice smiling at the private joke.

They laugh and cuddle each other remembering the past and their deep friendship that has continued over the years.

THE END

**Coming soon
Coffee Maidz Discoveries**

About the Author

Zoanna Valund

As a young women she spent time as a barista working part time in cafes and other outlets. Her day to day experiences inspired her to keep notes and a journal. Working as a barista and a server in many different cafes, her observations and recall built up insights which have inspired her writing . Her stories resonate with many who have read them privately as they capture some of the unseen and human aspects life in general.

Also by

By the same Publisher

BEBE – finding Love

The Twilighters – Road Trip

www.ingramcontent.com/pod-product-compliance
Lightning Source LLC
Chambersburg PA
CBHW021234020726
47498CB00008B/2836